DANJE

GITTE TAMAR

BTW LLC

To those who believe they are followed by bad luck, there is a greater purpose within the frustration of feeling stuck.

☠

The more inspiration you are meant to invoke, the larger the wave of darkness that will try to capsize your boat.

☠

Remember, the world needs you to stay afloat; just as you are, your destiny is far brighter than you know.

Acknowledgment

Hello to all,

Thank you to every last of you, whether your part was big or small.

Thank you to each of my family and friends; you already know who you are, so I will refrain from listing each of your specific names. Just know I will forever be thankful for each of you who gave me never-ending love and emotional support.

Thank you to all my readers for continuing this journey with me. I am forever indebted to you.

Sincerely,

Contents

One

THE STORM

1965, Louisiana

This mid-September day finds the air in the bayou oppressive and the sky grim and hardened.

Each cloud is swollen; their crème-tinted pillowy sides are bulging, ready to erupt. It is an early indication that a hurricane is approaching. Even though it appears to be starting the same way as the ones before, those in its path are unaware that it is unlike any other. The storm comes with an ominous prediction that it will soon be the largest in the state's history.

When the gusts of wind start their journey, plowing through the cypress trees surrounding the wharf, everyone evacuates from the water, taking refuge inside their homes. An uncomfortable static fills the air while the community prepares for its arrival. The mysterious current infiltrates the windowsills, causing the hair on the residents' arms to stand on end as they gather nervously around their televisions and radios, eagerly awaiting news updates about the impending storm. The scenery is unrecognizable; the usually lively businesses are now empty, and all the boats are secured to the dock.

St. Luc appears abandoned.

In the town renowned for shrimp harvesting, the harbor is usually bustling, filled with fishermen working their nets, but today, all that can be heard is the slap of the choppy water and the whistle of the wind.

As the storm's velocity worsens, bursts of warm pinwheels swoop down along the bayou's adjoining harbor, terrorizing a long line of docked shrimp and houseboats. As it ruffles the water beneath their bellies, their rocking hulls sway from side to side, jostling their outriggers and nets. Their wild pitching builds momentum, causing the vessels to crash violently into their moorings. Each collision challenges the dock's stability, jeopardizing the bridge to the simplistic civilization.

Besides shrimping, the town is also renowned for its fish market. A narrow brick-paved street runs down the middle of St. Luc, lined with older storefronts that cater to the trade. On Saturdays, the sidewalks overflow with stands from local vendors selling anything from books to crayfish. Even the local vodou practitioner sets up a stand occasionally, and customers line up around the block for potions and spells to help them gain fortune, health, love, or, on rare occasions, revenge.

Despite its overall energy resembling the laid-back vibe of a timeworn beach town, the Creole essence and French architecture give the backwater civilization an added charm. During the summer, its enchanting spirit attracts tourists who drive long distances to admire the main street's unique feel; its lively nature has become routine. People come from all over the country to view the avenue of historic wood and ironwork adorning the colorful buildings that encapsulate a mark in history the residents have worked hard to preserve.

Architecture is one of many things that draw outsiders' attention. As the luster of daylight winds down to the night, visitors sit by the dock to stargaze over the swamp, where troves of chirping crickets and alligators with glowing eyes set the enchanting scene.

The incoming storm darkens the sky above, and the bayou's inviting shimmer dissipates, sucking the magic away from the Louisiana town.

Every shop owner has already boarded their respective storefronts' windows except for Albert, who owns and operates the *A. Gilly's Bait Shop*.

During the last decade, Albert has taken over the family business. He views the opportunity as more of an obligation than an interest. In fact, the burden has made him resentful. He never intended to be trapped in the town, living out his father's legacy. He has dreamed since childhood of becoming a renowned trombonist and playing in clubs across Louisiana, and he will do whatever it takes to ensure that his children won't face the same unfulfilling fate.

The shop has been passed down through the Gilly family for three generations, and as the only child of his parents, it was Albert's responsibility to keep the family legacy alive. Until now, the establishment has operated seamlessly in the same fashion for the past seventy-five years.

His father's death led to a noticeable increase in difficulty for the store's operations. The constant struggle of managing building maintenance expenses and plummeting sales creates a lot of pressure on Albert, which spills over into his personal life, resulting in missed mortgage payments and conflicts with his spouse. Every aspect of his unfulfilling existence has felt like an uphill battle after his dad died, and it has nothing to do with missing the man.

Albert pessimistically questions if he has inherited his father's karmic debt along with the rest of the unwanted assets. His father's destructive behavior has profoundly affected him, and he often uses humor to cope. He has frequently joked that if the man had a century to make amends, he still wouldn't apologize for a goddamned thing—a sentiment he held until his unexpected death nearly ten years ago.

Albert only does what is necessary to bring in a paycheck, leaving maintenance tasks to be dealt with later due to indifference and lack of finances. When he was young, his parents deliberately did not assign him demanding jobs such as maintenance and storm preparation, which led to an inaccurate understanding of the responsibility. By the time he realized he had been tricked, his father had died, and he had a family to support, leaving him with no choice but to stay. Their decision to ill-prepare him became more of a hindrance for him in adulthood than a source of motivation.

Unfortunately for him, his family store is one of the few two-story buildings in town, giving it the most windows of any structure on the street.

Initially, while everyone else hammered plywood onto their storefronts to protect the glass panes, he laughed. As the owner, this is the first time he has faced a massive storm, and his lack of experience has caused him to delay the completion of boarding up the second-floor windows made of leaded glass. At first, he did not take the warnings of the weather's severity seriously and was convinced it would pass through without incident, like the storms before. But seeing things worsen makes him second-guess his assumptions, and he scrambles to get the rest of his shop ready in time.

He fights off the heavy rain from chilling him to the bone by wearing green wading overalls, tall rubber boots, and a tan fishing hat tucked beneath the hood of a heavy yellow raincoat. Stressed and in a hurry to finish, he tries to shield his body from the weather by pulling his hood tightly around his chocolate-toned cheeks and short, kinky, graying hair with his left hand while hammering with his right.

With only one window left on the second floor, he fights to keep his balance on the slippery rungs of his mud-smeared wooden ladder. He is teetering on the top, hammering as fast as possible.

Abruptly, hail pelts him from above; it resembles tiny marbles as it strikes the buildings' roofs and brick-lined streets. Albert shields his eyes from the icy assault. Luckily, he only has one piece left to secure. After pounding the final nail into the piece of plywood, he wastes no time scurrying to the ground. He struggles to keep the wind from snatching the ladder from his grip as he lays it down on the sidewalk.

Holding onto his hood with both hands, he scans the horizon to check the storm's progress; his jacket uncontrollably flaps away from his body, slapping his sides. "Lordy, Lordy," he says.

The clouds' hue has drastically shifted from dark gray to violet and green. Feeling the wind picking up speed around him, Albert glances toward the houseboats secured along the dock. His eyes lock on one at the end of the line.

The sky's unnatural glow reflects off the chipping navy blue paint, creating an eerie radiance around it. He inherited the dilapidated old floating structure from his father. The houseboat was the man's prized possession. He cherished it so much that he spent most of his nights on it instead of being with his family, just like his father did. Conversely, Albert has no sentimental connection to the ramshackle place and only thinks negatively about it.

His father made explicit that his houseboat was a sanctuary solely for him, and nobody was allowed to interrupt him there. Albert viewed it as a place where his father went to abandon him.

During his eighth-grade year, he vividly remembers seeking his father's guidance after devastatingly catching his first girlfriend making out with another boy behind the bleachers. Distraught, he gathered his courage and went to the houseboat for fatherly advice. He cautiously peered through the windows before knocking and saw a young woman—who was not his mother—stripped naked, lying on the couch.

Despite being only thirteen years old, he had enough understanding of the situation and his father's short fuse to know that disclosing the man's secret would result in dire consequences. He ran home, rushed inside, and never spoke a word to anyone, not even his mother, about what he had seen.

Since then, he has held a deep-seated hatred for the houseboat and deliberately avoids looking at it whenever he passes. The structure is an eyesore, a continuous reminder of his father's negative impact that still looms over him like a dark cloud, much like the gloomy mist hovering over its rusty tin roof.

Albert was determined not to follow his father's sinful ways. He preferred avoiding the man altogether. Instead of spending time with him, he dedicated himself to helping his mother, assisting her with chores to make up for his father's transgressions in the dilapidated shack. Although he didn't reveal anything he witnessed, he prioritized shielding her from the pain of his discovery.

His mother, born and raised in Haiti, was named Asefi at birth, which translates to 'enough girls.' Her parents chose the name as a plea to the spirits for a boy, which, to their dismay, never came.

In her mind, she was enough, so after migrating to Louisiana to marry, she chose a new name, Mambo.

Her pride in her immigrant roots led her to speak mostly Haitian Creole, the language of her birthplace. She refused to abandon her traditional clothing, opting for long cotton dresses with ruffles that swayed in the summer heat and a colorful tignon wrapped around her head. She was convinced that covering her skull would keep the lespri, or evil spirits, from possessing her pure intentions.

For added protection, she carried a small leather-bound book labeled *DANJE* with her. Albert had been taught since he was young that the word meant danger, and he knew not to touch it. His mother was the only one allowed to read what was inside.

Despite the difficulties presented by her narcissistic husband, she never had a negative thing to say and consistently expressed gratitude for the blessings in her life. Albert couldn't help but wonder if she had performed a protective spell or ritual from her book to sustain her positive outlook.

Even after his father's passing, she upheld her smile as she asked Albert to return his cremated ashes to the place he loved, the houseboat. According to her, it would allow him to rest peacefully in the afterlife.

At that instant, he revealed what he saw through the window - his father's infidelity. As she listened calmly, her smile became more pronounced. Then, lifting a finger to his lips, she motioned for silence. "Nou se lanme, nouu pa kenbe kras. We are like the sea; we wash away the dirt." She said.

He realized by her reaction that she had been aware all along and was in disbelief over her ability to maintain compassion for the man after years of mistreatment. Even though Albert's sentiment toward the man differed, he agreed to do what she asked out of love for her.

As she passed him his father's remains, she stared directly into his eyes and whispered, "Mwen priye Bondye va pwoteje nan tout malè. I pray God will protect you from all danger."

Regardless of her words of encouragement, he still dreaded the walk to the houseboat. Upon entering, he quickly fulfilled his obligation, only staying long enough to drop off his cremated remains and turn off the lights. "There you go, you son of a bitch. Now you can stay in here twenty-four-seven with all your dirty little secrets," he said as he locked the door. From that day on, he has only entered when necessary, with work gloves and a flashlight to reset a breaker after a storm. As he stares at the dock, he ponders the challenges brought on him by his unsolicited existence; he wishes for his father's prized possession to vanish into the swamp's depths, but it remains afloat, unscathed, and mocking him.

The unsightly floating structure, with its tin roof shrouded in a misty haze, reminds him of his father's adverse impact, which looms over him like a dark cloud. Even after a decade, he still wonders how his mother survived his father's destructive behavior.

Albert's superstitious leanings stemmed from his upbringing by a mother with Haitian ancestry and a belief in vodou. The bedtime stories she told Albert always included a moral lesson; her favorite topic was karma. She would caution that one's behavior will affect their reincarnated life, their children, and their children's children.

She often told a tale about a terrible man who enlisted a vodou practitioner to perform a nefarious ritual to transfer his debt to an unsuspecting individual. The unwilling recipients of his karmic debt varied with each telling and ranged from his estranged wife to a difficult neighbor. Whenever she recounted the story, his mother would chuckle and emphasize that there were no shortcuts to avoiding punishment for bad behavior.

Based on his endless misfortune, he often wondered if he was the unlucky recipient of his father's karmic debt.

Looking up, Albert says, "I'm not sure where my old man is hiding, but if someone up there is listening, please let this damn wind blow his bad karma back to him for my kids and me. Any help you can provide is much appreciated. Hallelujah, Amen!"

A dense, murky fog creeps up the home's sides as it rolls in over the water; the hail from above turns into heavy rain. Something about the mysterious nature of the iridescent presence gives him hope that everything will be fine.

Taking the slight shift in weather as validation that his request has been heard, he watches the wind batter the sides of the houseboat's worn shingles, and the waves rattle the structure's platform.

In unison, the emergency sirens stationed throughout the fishing town loudly sound. The blaring echoes warn everyone to take shelter in their homes, cautioning the hurricane's escalation.

Albert stumbles over his feet. The brash, high-pitched squeal startles him. As he clutches onto his chest to calm his racing heart, his attention shifts to the lightning flashing across the sky. "Shit," he says, realizing that he has run out of time.

Because of his earlier procrastination in boarding up the shop, he has no time to evacuate and cannot reach home before the storm's peak. "I guess I gotta take my chances and shelter in the store. There is not a damn thing I can do about it now. If the wind blows the thing away with me in it, I'll just have to roll with it." He says as he peers up at his store's sign.

At once, nature's elements rage with aggression, blowing harder, tearing off the shingles of the neighboring hat shop. As the storm approaches, he feels an eerie sensation of being watched from the dark windows of the houseboat.

The wind's boldness makes him lose his balance. As he stumbles uncontrollably, his footing slips, and he grabs the shop siding. Acting fast, he catches himself to stop his fall and, getting his final gripping, clutches onto the handle of his locked storefront to steady himself.

A sweeping gust picks up the ladder near the toes of his boots. His eyes widen in disbelief as it effortlessly tumbles in a spiraling vortex down the brick street. Concerned he will be next, he frantically turns to unlock the shop door to get inside, but something catches his attention.

A homeless man is lying across the street on the sidewalk; he looks to be in his twenties. Tightly huddled in a blanket to keep warm, the material slightly shields him from the elements; lethargic, he is unaware of the danger.

Albert cannot understand how someone can sleep through the tremulous weather. "What the hell?" he says. Though he is in a hurry, he visualizes that being his son, and out of good conscience, he waits a moment to watch him before going inside. Not seeing any movement, he assumes the man must be dead. "Huh. Well, I guess that makes better sense."

It may seem morbid, but his unfazed reaction is typical in the community; he has been desensitized to death, like others living there.

Since St. Luc's location is remote, it has become a hub for wandering drifters escaping their demons. It's common for bodies to be discovered in the swamp, as many fail to flee what torments them. The sight of death is nothing of a surprise; more than anything, residents view it as a reminder to count their blessings for being alive.

Just as he is ready to turn around, he spots one of the man's feet escaping from underneath the comforter. Shaken by the realization that he is alive, he yells to get the man's attention. "Hey, you've got to get up! Do you hear me? There's a storm coming!"

The blasts of humid air worsen, each gust more powerful than the last, breaking miscellaneous pieces off the storefronts' roofs.

A section of wooden gable is torn from the top of a shop a few doors down and thrown into the street, barely missing the homeless man's legs, but he does not flinch.

Albert holds on tighter to the doorknob to keep from blowing away while covering his head to dodge the debris. Nervous about the stranger's safety, he yells louder, trying to make his voice heard through the howling wind. "Come on, now! Get up! You've got to listen to me! You are going to die if you stay out here! We only have moments left before things get real ugly! If you get up now, you can shelter inside my shop!"

The man remains still; he is not responding.

Becoming anxious, Albert fidgets; his eyes drift to the path he would take to rescue the man, but his memory of the ladder thrown through the street stops him. He cannot help thinking of his family waiting back home and what they would do if something happened to him; they would have no one to provide for them. The thought of them being homeless like the young man fills him with a sense of dread.

Each gust of wind propels the rain sideways, creating a watery blur in the air. It pelts Albert's exposed cheek, making the skin raw; he knows he must take shelter. Unable to hold on, his weakening arm loosens its grip. His guilt continues to overwhelm him. "Lord, forgive me for what I'm about to do," he whispers.

"I gotta get inside! If you can hear me, take cover in the houseboat at the end of the dock!" he shouts. As much as he feels terrible about his decision, he does not look back.

Using the last of his strength, he fights his way into the building. The wind forcefully slams the door shut behind him, causing the bell at the top of the door frame to ring wildly. The noise of the high-pitched clanging, combined with the continuing sounds of sirens, is deafening. Quickly locking the door behind himself, Albert moves through the shop and takes refuge under a table securely bolted to the floor.

At that exact moment, the homeless man stirs. Waking up to the commotion, his eyes spring open, and his irises dilate. Believing the siren's sound is from a police car, he becomes frightened and covers his head with the comforter. He hyperventilates as he lifts the torn fabric from his face to peer around.

Varied debris, torn from buildings, tumbles down the street.

Unaware of what is happening, his bloodshot eyes dart to the fronts of the boarded-up shops around him. His twitching fingers tighten their grip around the blanket, and in a foggy daze, he incoherently fights the wind to stagger to his feet.

The storm continues without mercy.

As he labors to remain upright, his emaciated body is tested by a gust of wind catching beneath the tattered cover around his frail frame. His reflexes are slow, and he is late to react to the weather's sudden escalation. As he attempts to hang onto the fabric, his body is thrown into the side of the building. His hands lose their grip, and he watches the blanket fly into the sky to join the swirling clouds. The lack of coverage against the wind exposes his dark skin to the elements, revealing that his body is covered in varying shades of bruises, ranging from purple to black.

The progressing storm turns his surroundings into a disconsolate shade of gray. Everything resembles an apocalyptic movie, and he thinks he is hallucinating. Wanting answers, he looks past the dirt stains covering his light blue jeans to his bare feet, then at his distorted surroundings. Each shifting position exhibits his elbows sticking out from his once-white ragged shirt. Discolorations on the underside of each forearm reveal the needle tracks from heroin use.

As he attempts to regain his bearings, the sight of the chaos only leaves him more confused. He does not know where he is; each building remains unfamiliar. He stares into the distance, trying to recollect how he got to the town.

A blood-orange glow is cast over the tops of the skyline, making the buildings appear sinister and uninviting. His fear is magnified by the imagery's ominous tone, causing him to flinch at every sound of crashing metal and *whoosh* of swirling debris.

The wind blows harder, thrusting trash cans and portions of wooden structures down the street. A soaring staircase railing narrowly misses his head as he grabs onto anything he can to stabilize himself from being carried away while scanning his surroundings for shelter. "Hello, is anyone there?" he shouts.

The rain transitions to a wave of hail pelting the ground. While he surveys the desolation of the thoroughfare and sidewalks, the rows of buildings' heights fluctuate around him like bouncing springs. "Come on, man, what did you take?" he says. He rubs his eyes.

As the elements worsen, the loud crashes from boats colliding with each other and their moorings become more frequent, conflicting with the siren's rhythm and adding to the mayhem.

The grating noises feed his paranoia. Panicked, he hyperventilates. "Help! Someone, help me!" he shouts. There is no response but the roar of the howling storm.

His heart races. Convinced that something is out to get him, he tries to run, but the wind blows him back into the side of the building.

He cannot focus, his eyes darting to every dark shadow and boarded-up shop. Caught up in his paranoid spiral, he grabs a fistful of his matted curls so tightly that the front of his head throbs. "They've shut me out. They ... they have left me for dead. I can't let it get me. I have to find a place to hide." He cries.

Despite not knowing what he is running from, he knows he must get somewhere safe. His eyes shift toward the row of houseboats. There is one on the far end without boarded-up windows that strikes him as less uninviting than the others; its worn navy paint calls to him as it glistens under the sky's eerie orange-green haze.

He takes a deep breath and releases a grunt as he combats the wind to make his way toward the dock. Each forceful gust ferociously funnels over the water, whipping through the boats and boathouses.

As he steps onto the pier, the wooden surface shifts beneath his bare feet. The storm pushes against his chest, its velocity knocking him onto his hands and knees. Crawling, he clutches onto the underside of the wooden planks, holding himself to the dock while inching ahead. Board by board, he pulls himself toward his only hope, the row of houseboats.

As the hail brews in the clouds, pelting the earth, it mixes with the angry swamp water, creating a wet, icy sheath that covers the dock. Shivering, he continues to crawl.

The storm rages out of control, creating giant waves that sweep over the floating pathway, drenching his body and wrinkling his skin.

As he forces himself to keep moving through the icy pain, he notices that each rolling wave carries sets of large, glowing eyes. Seeing what he is sure is lurking alligators makes him recoil in terror. He screams, but the storm masks his plea.

Layers of fog fill the swamp, making it impossible to tell which direction he is going.

The wind blows harder, pushing a tsunami-like wave over the dock. It carries a massive alligator that skids on its belly across the boards, snapping at the man's feet as it passes before sliding off the other side.

Scared and sobbing, he refocuses on his survival; he shakes his terror by fixating on the only outline of a houseboat he can spot through the horrible conditions. Albert's father's timeworn home stands out as his only salvation; the wind erratically causes the door's screen to slam open and shut as if signaling him to come near.

Hoping the wooden entry is unlocked, he mutters a prayer while pulling himself to the front of the rickety shack. Barely able to control his unsteadiness from exhaustion, he drags himself onto the porch, almost tumbling into the water.

The screen's movement becomes increasingly hostile as he approaches. Reaching out, he grabs the doorframe to steady himself. He twists the old brass handle on the wooden entrance and hears the latch's reassuring *click*. The wind fights him as he tries to pull it open, and as it finally gives way, the hurricane surges him inside.

The door slams shut behind him. With little strength remaining, his shaking hands lock it, and he immediately falls to the floor and curls into a tight ball.

The inside is musty and completely dark; the building appears as if it has been abandoned for years. Layers of dust and cobwebs cover the vintage interior, preserved in time.

His legs slowly regain feeling because of the slight increase in warmth from the outside air filtering into the drafty room. He refuses to let go of his knees as he lies on the floor and acclimates to the idea that he has done the impossible and reached safety.

He inhales deeply, feeling relieved. There is a potent stench, and subtle hints of rotten meat and spoiled milk accent the stagnant air. It sparks his curiosity. He is ready to explore and slowly stands while slightly bending his knees to brace himself against the choppiness of the waves.

Unable to see, he fumbles through the space, patting the walls to find a light switch. His fingers touch the button near the front door and push it, but nothing happens. The room remains dark.

An icy shiver runs down his spine. It's as if someone is blowing frigid air on the back of his neck. He nervously shrugs. "Still better than being on the streets. Anything beats that," he says. "I'm just lucky to have gotten to this pad." He brushes off the inconvenience and extends his hands out to continue feeling around him. "There has got to be another light around here somewhere."

The layout of the houseboat is simplistic. Near the front door is a living room area that opens into a kitchen. Down a short hallway, there's a single bedroom with a bathroom.

After finding his way to the dimly lit kitchen, he fumbles mindlessly, his hands grazing the empty counters. The sound of clinking metal fills the air as the boat rocks violently. His eyes light up with excitement as he searches for a drawer knob and pulls it open with both hands.

As he reaches inside, his fingertips trace the familiar shape of a spoon, confirming that he's found the silverware drawer. The waves underneath the floorboards rock harder.

Overzealous, he continues to reach further to the back of the cubby, and a sharp object jabs the tip of his finger. "Damn it," he says, quickly retracting his hand. He winces as he shoves the wounded digit into his mouth, tasting the metallic tang of blood. Realizing that he must have touched a knife, he slams the drawer.

Suddenly, a lightning bolt strikes overhead, causing the windows to flash with a blinding intensity. Significant fits of thunder follow, their proximity shaking the boat.

The jarring movements and strobing lights make him disoriented. As the ship rocks, he braces himself by clutching onto the counter and hits his hip on the drawer front, discovering something hard in his pocket.

It is a lighter.

He grins. "Thank you, lady luck," he says.

In the past, he was always one to borrow lighters from his dealers, but recently, he had an experience that took a dangerous turn when one of them threatened his life for asking. Not wanting to make the same mistake again, he used the last of his panhandling money to purchase his own.

Pulling the brass Zippo lighter from his pocket, he spins the small metal wheel to ignite a flame. "Come on," he says. His pride turns to frustration as he continues to create useless friction.

Small sizzles leave the top, followed by tiny sparks that dissipate; there is no fluid. The smell of burned smoke makes him irritable. He does not want to admit to failing to fill the container. Convinced that the wave soaking him earlier has made it a dud, he flicks his finger faster, projecting his rage onto the lever. "Piece of shit," he says. The rapid pace causes his flesh to rub raw, and he throws the lighter across the room.

As it skips across the floor, a gas lantern secured to a small table in the corner flickers simultaneously.

Conflicted, he looks at his hands. He is convinced he has something to do with it. "How the hell?" he says. He pivots toward the living room to face the direction of the light.

As the flame engulfs the lantern's wick, the warm glow exposes more of the space's attributes, including a green velvet paisley loveseat.

Anxiously chuckling to rid himself of his nerves, he glances at the flickering flame. "Well, beggars can't be choosers," he says. Then, timing his steps with the rolling waves, he sprints for the couch and sits. "Got to say, this is a nice setup someone's got here." He cannot recall the last time he's had the luxury of sitting on furniture as he shimmies into the cushion and leans back to get comfortable.

The wind wails through the structure's walls as the hurricane's eye shifts over the swamp. Its whistling sound is so piercing that it seems it could shatter the windows.

The unrelenting noise, paired with the dissipation of his high, feeds his unease. His heart pounds, and sweat trickles down his forehead as he attempts to ignore his growing paranoia. "Where is it? " He says. Unable to take the throbbing palpitations and nausea, he closes his eyes to focus, frantically searching his pockets and pulls out a small makeshift envelope made from aluminum foil. With a quivering smirk, he leans over the sofa's arm and holds the silver object in the light to look at it. "Hello, my friends." He says.

Pills, powder, and paper bounce around in the tinfoil as he gives it a little shake. Opening the packet, he pours a mixture into the palm of his hand. "Tomorrow, I'll wake up and put all this shit behind me. Then, I'm outta here. No harm, no foul," he says. He dry-swallows the items with a grimace, struggling with their unpleasant taste and textures. "That's the good stuff." He says.

The light beside him brightly flickers.

He glances toward it and laughs. "Yeah, you know what I'm talking about," he says. Knowing he has little time before the high kicks in, he scoots lower into a slouched position, allowing his body to sink deeper into the couch. As his head lies on the back cushion, he shuts his eyes, imagining the gas lamp as a fireplace. He can feel a light warmth against his cheek. "This must be what they mean by living that high life," he says.

A flash of lightning strikes closer to the rickety house, and the thunder worsens. Focusing on the heavily rocking boat, he yawns. Rather than feeling anxious, the pitching soothes him. Each sway propels his mind into a deeper trance.

As he relinquishes control, his consciousness slips away; the darkness engulfs him, and everything falls silent.

THE FOOL

Two

THE
COMEDOWN

Nearing the end of the drug's lifespan, his fingers twitch and his eyes flutter open.

Unsure of the time, he looks to the porthole window in the room and flinches. The bright sunrise blinds him.

Each bird chirping outside sounds muffled through the thin walls.

With a fog still clouding his mind, the glimmering light feels like a nuisance. He is nowhere near ready to get up and rolls over to shield his eyes. "I can't believe it is already morning," he says.

Although the daylight should be a joyful sight, something about it feeds an eerie sensation lurking in the room's air. Not giving it much thought, he yawns and takes a moment to absorb his surroundings.

As he reaches behind his head, he feels the softness of a pillow underneath his sore neck; a layer of thin cotton sheets drapes his body. The material lightly tickles his chest. Its crisp, unsoiled texture is unfamiliar. Startled, he flails his arms to fight the covering away from his upper body, and upon realizing what it is, he chuckles and takes a deep breath to calm his racing heart. He can't remember the last time he felt the comfort of a bed or the touch of a clean blanket.

The piercing squawks of a blue heron outside penetrate the walls, diverting his attention from his thoughts. Despite enjoying the bed's coziness, nothing about the scene mirrors his once familiar environment; everything feels off.

Although he wishes to bask in the luxury of having a pillow under his head, he can't shake a grimy sensation stemming from his underlying amnesia. He struggles to wake up at a faster rate. "Think," he says. "How did you get here?"

He tries recalling what occurred before his haze set in the night before, but his mind has no memory after the moment of taking a seat on the street. His last recollection is wrapping the comforter around himself and lying on the cold ground. After reflecting on the drugs he had taken, he recalls purchasing his fix from a new dealer and laughs it off. "I guess he wasn't bluffing. That was some powerful shit," he says. "Hell, that would take out an elephant."

The sunlight flickers through the window's glass as the cloud coverage shifts in the sky. He winces; it triggers a flashback to the lightning, and with no memory of the previous night's experience, he is unaware of why he is panicking.

A headache sets in as he runs his tongue against the fronts of his teeth to clear his mind. "He didn't warn me about the comedown," he says. He swallows to fight the dryness of his mouth and senses a cold draft blowing under the sheets; it caresses his skin.

The sensation makes him feel violated, causing his stomach to drop. As the tickling sends cold prickles down his spine, his breathing speeds up, provoking him to hyperventilate. He reluctantly peeks under the sheet and throws it back down to cover himself.

All his clothes are missing.

"What the..." he says. His eyes widen. He takes another look and is met with the same reality. It leaves him in shock. "Come on, snap out of it. Think of your last steps." He pulls the covers up to his neck to compensate for the lack of clothing; his embarrassment makes his mind flutter, and he can't process his thoughts. Still unable to remember anything, he grunts with shameful confusion over his nakedness.

He attempts to shake his insecurities over what may have happened. "Focus. Come on, focus," he says as a puff of air leaves his nostrils. His jaw clenches angrily. "When I get my hands on whoever did this ... Oh, boy."

Attempting to calm himself, he takes a deep breath to clear his nerves, but as hard as he tries to get his mind straight, his recollection is the same. His memory is a void after sitting on the street the night before, and the unknown fills him with unease. The emotion causes his heartbeats to become irregular; he has a disgust with himself that he has never felt before.

Everything about the idea of getting taken advantage of is unnerving to him. The possibility of a stranger pulling the wool over his eyes fills him with anger and fuels his frustration. Unable to control his boiling emotions, he snaps. "Motherfucker!" he says. "Where are you? Show your face."

He sits straight up and lifts his hands, forming fists in front of his chin, ready to fight. Trying to find whoever did this to him, he scans the room for the perpetrator.

The cloud coverage turns dense outside, engulfing the houseboat and casting darkness over its interior. Everything is silent. He is alone.

His heavy breathing slows as he works to control its pace and mask his nerves. Even though he wants to kill whoever has put him in such a precarious situation, the lack of response eases his mind. Releasing a sigh, he takes a moment to center himself.

He shifts his weight under the covers to get more comfortable and notices something cold resting against his right ankle.

The icy feeling of it reminds him of something familiar—an ankle monitor. He shivers as he thinks of his time in juvie for narcotics possession, and the unease makes his intestines churn. Wanting to forget the memory and resolute in not allowing his fear to get the best of him, he pulls the covers up to his chin and analyzes his surroundings for a way out.

A thick layer of dust coats the room; the only thing not affected is the bed. Based on the place's condition, it is apparent that the space has not been lived in for some time. Beneath the grime, the room's decor appears trapped in time, exuding fifties-era vibes. No wallpaper accentuates the walls—just wood paneling complemented by modest, well-worn furniture.

Gripping the sheet, he edges his way to the side of the bed, but he is met by the resistance of the metal around his right ankle; he is stuck. Desperate to free himself, he pulls with all his strength against the restraint, his heart racing with adrenaline from the fear of being trapped.

With each tug, harder than the last, the metal links clink together underneath the thin sheet.

He lifts the fabric from his leg to investigate what binds him. A heavily rusted chain, attached to a shackle secured around his ankle, leads to the bedpost.

The sight of the padlock causes his forehead to sweat as the thought sinks in that he is held captive. In desperation, he gives another pull, and the force causes the dull edge of the cuff to tear into his dry skin. The sudden onset of pain triggers him to grab his leg and look down to check his injury. He notices the effort has unraveled more of the links. His eyes widen, and his attention quickly diverts from the gash upon realizing there is enough leeway for his bare feet to touch the floor.

Scooting himself to the edge of the mattress, he places his feet flat on the ground, the mustard-shag carpet wedging between his toes. He grabs the chain and tugs at it with all his might. His thought of liberation is fleeting, as he finds the restraint is firmly fixed to the bedframe and taut at the end of its slack.

The absence of freedom causes his panic to resurface, and he frantically scans the room, intending to kill whoever did this to him.

Assuming the sicko who stripped him nude and chained him to the bed must be somewhere in the home, he yells loud enough for his captor to hear him. "If you're after money, you picked the wrong guy. I'm flat broke," he says. Laughing sarcastically, he continues, "I'll make you a deal. If you cut me some slack and let me go, we can forget about this whole thing; I swear I'm not a snitch. All you gotta do is unlock me, and you won't hear from me again. "

Waiting for a response, he only hears one voice carrying through the cabin and echoing back to his ears. It is his own.

The silence eats him alive.

Over his lifetime on the streets, he's heard many stories of people gone missing, and each ended the same: with the person never being heard from again. The thought of being tortured or becoming another statistic triggers his distress; he cannot stand the idea that he has no control over his destiny. His unease makes him sweat profusely, and the saltiness of his perspiration dripping down his forehead stings as it trickles into his eyes.

The silence feels like an eternity, and he can't take it anymore. He is at the end of his patience but fights his urge to speak, giving himself a few more minutes to listen for any sign of life. His eyes dart around the room. Every second without words, the thoughts infiltrating his mind become more negative. As his clammy forehead goes pale, his toes tap against the carpet. "So, what's your answer?" he asks.

Everything remains stagnant.

"Well?" he asks. "I think it's a pretty good deal, wouldn't you say?"

Waiting for a response feels like a lifetime.

As his impatience grows, his eyes twitch. "I know you can hear me," he says.

The relentless silence causes his desperation to worsen. Clearing his throat, he diverts his attention to the shackle. He knows that if he has any hope of survival, freeing himself is the only option, and to do that, and he must create a diversion to cover the noise of trying to pick the lock.

His hands stretch toward his ankle to fiddle with the iron cuff, and concurrently, he raises his voice to hide what he is doing. "Come on, man, this isn't funny. We both are grown-ass adults, so let's act like it," he says; his nerves quicken his speech. He anxiously laughs. "Hell, I will make you a deal. If you let me go now, I'll help you find someone worth your time—someone with money. What do you say about that, huh?"

The room remains still.

Believing he is getting close to opening the lock, his fingers shake, and he speaks louder. "I know your kind and what you're after. You want cash, and there's nothing wrong with that. I would do the same, but you are out of luck. I'm gonna be honest with you: I'm nothing more than a broke junkie, and that's a fact. I don't have a pot to piss in." He tries to get his point across without feeling completely worthless by making light of his tragic narrative, shaking his head, and laughing it off; he continues, "Shit, no one would pay a penny of ransom for my ass. It's true. No one cares enough to miss me. Most of the people I know have been hauled off to jail for nothing more than existing. But, hey..."

A loud *thump* cuts off his rant; it's coming from the window.

The abrupt noise startles him to silence. He twists around and spots a pair of fluttering black wings falling out of view. "It's just a bird," he says. As he watches it fly away, he notices the sunlight has gotten brighter and gets an idea. Even though he cannot see another home through the glass, he figures a neighbor should be up or someone should be walking outside. He screams at the top of his lungs. "Help! Someone help me! I'm trapped in here. Some damn psychos got me chained to the bed! Help!"

A loud thud resonates from the hallway; something is scuffling outside the bedroom door.

His eyes widen, and his heart races. Immediately, his attention turns to the entrance, and he falls silent to listen.

The methodical thumping sounds make the identity of the noise obvious—it's footsteps.

In disbelief, he lowers himself to the carpet for a better look. Placing his cheek against the musty shag rug, he squints, watching for a sign of feet through the gap under the door.

He sees what appears to be the shadow of someone pacing the hallway.

Nervously clearing his throat, he scrambles to apologize. "You know I didn't mean what I said. I didn't even know anyone was in here."

The treading stops; someone is listening.

His anxiety intensifies, taking the lack of movement as a bad sign. Worried he has upset whomever his captor is, he scrambles to remedy the situation. "I can be hushed if that's what you want. You're the boss; I will be quiet as a church mouse if you dig silence. He tries to remain silent, but his captor's lack of response triggers him. "Man, I didn't mean to say anything that would offend you. I'm just telling it like it is. You got to know being left in here naked is real heavy for me."

In response, a muffled voice sounds from the hallway. Even though he cannot understand anything being said, he feels like he is getting somewhere. Sighing with relief, he knows it may be his only opportunity and pushes harder to convince the person to set him free; he must connect with whoever is on the other side of the door.

"My name is Adonis, Ad—Adonis Landry. I was born to a single mom, Denise. I didn't get to spend much time with her since she left when I was eight, but it seemed like people liked her. Um ... what else?" he says.

He becomes nervous and pats the floor while he looks around the room, trying to think of more facts to share. With each whap of his hand, the carpet dispels small dust clouds that fill the air. As debris drifts underneath his nose, it enters his lungs, and he uncontrollably coughs.

His inability to breathe without hacking causes him to become uncomfortably flustered. The last thing he wants to do is recall more of his past, and he shakes his head to cut off his thoughts. "To be honest, I don't remember much from my upbringing besides being homeless for most of my life. That's the one thing I know," he says.

Everything becomes still on the other side of the door, and the muttering stops.

In a panic, he fears his prospects of being freed from the shackle are diminishing. He talks faster, giving one last plea. "C'mon, man, let's cut the crap. We are both people. Just come in here and let me go."

A loud rumble sounds from a rusty vent mounted on the wall behind him. It is immediately followed by a powerful gust of cold air exiting the slats. As he stares at the door, he flinches as the icy breeze blowing on his bare shoulder sends shivers down his spine.

The movement in the hallway resumes, now with a rustling sound instead of the heavy thud of footsteps.

Suddenly, the room is filled with the metallic chime as something is flicked under the door. His eyes widen as the object skips across the bedroom's grassy carpet and stops near his foot.

With the sheet wrapped around himself, he frantically combs the shag rug and, upon finding the item, seizes it. His fingers tremble as he opens his grasp and tries to get a steady look.

Realizing it is a skeleton key, he peers at the hole in the shackle around his ankle and scrambles to see if it will fit.

It is a match.

In disbelief over the sudden turn of events, he laughs with relief. "Thanks, man. You won't regret this. I knew we could figure this out," he says. With a twist of the key, the locking mechanism clicks, and his eyes light up with excitement as the iron falls to the floor.

He rubs his ankle to ease the pain caused by the restraint. " You know, people like us, the underdog types, gotta stick together." He says.

There is no reply.

The rattling sound of the cooling system kicking on cuts through the awkward quiet. Not wanting to push his luck,

Adonis jumps to his feet. His legs feel weak beneath him. In a rush, he wraps the sheet around himself like a toga while scanning the room for his clothes. Not seeing them, his eyes shift to the door. "Say, can you tell me where to find my pants? I want to get dressed so my bare ass cheeks aren't hanging out. It's cold in here," he says.

Suddenly, an eerie creak catches his attention. The wall's wood paneling shifts, exposing a hidden closet.

Freaked out by the unexpected movement, he jumps and grips the fabric tighter for security. Despite being unsure of the secret door, his curiosity gets the best of him, and he cautiously approaches it to get a better look. As he gets closer, he whispers under his breath, "This situation keeps getting weirder by the minute." He raises his voice to get the attention of whoever is in the hallway. "Are the clothes behind the door?" he asks.

Rather than an answer, he is met with the sound of departing footsteps.

Adonis looks at the room's exit, then back to the newly opened access before him; taking a deep breath, he cautiously grabs the edge of the paneling and pulls it open. "I'm going to take that as a yes," he says.

The inside of the small square room is pitch black, smelling of mothballs and musty cedar. While reaching his hand inside, Adonis waves the stench away from his nose, and his fingers brush against a chain hanging from the ceiling. Swiftly, he pulls down on it; a single light bulb turns on.

As it illuminates the interior, he can see that the back of the large closet is filled with impeccably hung clothes. Intrigued by his discovery, he sifts through the dress shirts and suits, sniffing each to see if they are clean. They emit a subtle aroma of mildew.

Accustomed to not having regular access to a washer and dryer, the smell does not bother him; in fact, Adonis finds its familiarity oddly comforting. As he eyes the rich-looking fabrics, his fingers stop and linger over a specific pair of pants. The expensive-looking items are captivating; he has never been close to anything so luxurious.

Typically, he would not say a word before taking something, but given the circumstances, he turns toward the bedroom door and says, "I don't know why you needed me. By the looks of it, you must have plenty of dough. I've never seen so many fine threads."

Unable to keep his sticky fingers at bay, he grabs a pair of gray tweed pants with matching suspenders and a white dress shirt from their hangers. While pulling them on, he talks louder. "You don't mind if I borrow a few items, do you? I will give them right back after I find my clothes. It'll be so quick; you won't even notice your stuff missing." He has no intention of giving them back. On the contrary, he envisions himself parading through town after his escape, dressed in his new attire.

Like before, the room is quiet, aside from the clatter of the ventilation system.

He takes the absence of the word *no* as his permission to continue getting dressed.

With a broad smile on his face, Adonis eagerly continues to rummage, anticipating the discovery of more treasures. He spots a row of felt hats with colorful feathers hanging on the wall near a shelf lined with expensive dress loafers.

The flashy pieces leave him awestruck, marveling at their beauty.

Two items stand out to him, compelling him to snatch them up - a pair of white snakeskin mules and a matching hat. "I'm sure he won't mind," he says, slipping on the shoes and adjusting the fedora on his head. "I mean, It's the least he can do after what that man just put me through."

Adonis is in awe of how everything fits him flawlessly, confirming his conviction that these items are meant to be his. He feels fancy as he runs his fingers through the peacock feather in his cap.

A *bang* sounds, and the ventilation system's cold air stops blowing. The unanticipated noise causes him to halt what he is doing, reminding him that his captor is still in the home.

Adonis shakes his head and quietly chuckles as he looks back toward the bedroom door. "Okay. All you gotta do is get out of this place. That should be easy enough," he says. "You've dealt with the worst of the worst before. I mean, how bad can he be? He is a coward that refuses to show his damn face."

Feeling confident, he creeps closer to the door and stops to listen for footsteps. There is no sign of movement; his ears are met with silence.

Fighting off the last of his nerves, he places his hand on the doorknob, and the cold transfers from the metal to his skin. "Easy does it. All you gotta do is run," he says. Waiting for a moment, he leaves his ear pressed against the wood to listen.

Nothing changes. Everything remains oddly tranquil, but rather than putting him at peace; it prompts skepticism. He twists the handle and pauses, noticing there is no resistance. He finds it strange that it's not locked. "Huh..." he says. Though he thinks it odd, he seizes his moment to escape. "Time to get the hell out of here."

Taking a deep breath, he flings the door open and sprints down the hallway, not looking back. He spots daylight entering from under the home's front entry, sending narrow rays of light across the floor. His vision blurs into a tunnel-like path to his freedom.

As he enters the living room, he laughs at the stark contrast from the dismal room he just fled. Sunlight enters through the windows, casting warmth on the dingy furniture and countertops and illuminating the airborne dust. Even though something about his escape appears seamless, almost too effortless, it does not concern him. He is just relieved that his captor is not trying to stop him and is nowhere to be found. Instead, his uncontested escape is exciting, filling him with adrenaline, as if he were getting away with murder.

He flings the front door open, and a strong wind pushes against his chest. Holding the hat to his head, he shuts his eyelids and inhales the fresh breeze blowing across the water. It makes him grin; finally, he is free.

The air is filled with the sound of chirping birds as they swarm overhead.

He reaches to pull the door closed and opens his gaze, peering at the terrain before him. The sight stops him dead in his tracks, buckling his knees. "No, no, no, that's not right," he says.

The house is surrounded by murky water; the comfort of the dock is gone. There is no civilization in sight.

It appears the houseboat has drifted away down the bayou.

Gripped by fear, he holds onto the doorknob for dear life as he experiences a slight rocking sensation under his feet. His heart rate spikes, and he scoots backward to distance himself from the porch's edge.

The sun shines brightly overhead as a gentle breeze casts ripples across the calm waters.

As he investigates the distance, he sees nothing but a continuous swamp. There is no sign of land or any form of civilization.

Shielding his eyes, he scans the horizon again. Not a single trace of humanity exists.

Convinced that he is hallucinating, he slaps his cheek. "No way, man," he says, staring at the never-ending marsh. Sensing his loss of control, he panics and scurries back into the floating house to gather his thoughts.

Shutting the door behind him, he closes his eyes. "Come on, man. You can't just float off to nowhere. That's not possible. Let's try this one more time," he says. "Yeah, everything will be just fine."

He turns around and takes a deep breath in preparation to exit again, but as he reaches for the knob, he senses something watching him. The feeling stops him dead in his tracks and sends a shiver down his spine.

His suspicion is quickly validated by the sound of footsteps entering the kitchen and the opening of a drawer.

The noise triggers epinephrine to flood his system, and he shouts over his shoulder to stand his ground. "I can hear you in there. You stay back, do you hear me? I'm only going to warn you once, man. That's it before I beat your ass!"

Abruptly, the air falls quiet, filled only with an uncomfortable static.

Adonis has no interest in staying any longer. Taking a deep breath, he twists the handle. "You better not fucking follow me," he says.

He closes his eyes as if wishing himself into a different place, and then, flinging the door open, he exits.

A flock of seagulls squawks as they fly overhead.

His body shudders at the sound of the door slamming behind him. Reluctantly, he opens his eyes to observe his freedom but is met with the same murky water of the endless swamp.

It is a never-ending backdrop, filled with cypress trees, and spans as far as the eye can see in every direction; there is no escape. Adonis's eyes widen. He trembles at the sight as terror grows within him. "Oh, hell no," he says.

As he struggles to process his distress, the house hits a current, causing water to splash onto the porch. Worried it will stain his white snakeskin shoes, he hops back against the shingle siding of the rickety structure to dodge the wet surge.

He turns to look at the front door. Although his captor is inside, he determines that confronting him is better than staying outdoors, given that he has never learned to swim and believes that anything is better than drowning. In a state of panic, he hastily clutches the doorknob, only to hear the latch click from the other side, suggesting he is locked out.

Being stuck outside on the dilapidated porch fills him with dread. Suddenly, his ears are filled with the sound of something splashing in the water; he cautiously turns around to look.

THE HANGED MAN

Three

SNAPPING JAWS

The throng of seagulls becomes dense overhead, their cries filling the air.

Their presence causes his knees to quiver beneath him. Clenching his jaw, his childhood memories boil to the surface, and his thoughts spiral. He braces himself against the exterior siding to regain stability. His gaze shifts higher into the sky; there are more gulls than he remembered.

As the horde of birds swarm together out of thin air, they form a circling ring above him, like a pack of ravenous vultures.

Their spectacle takes his attention away from the splashing swamp water in the distance.

Worried about the flock's unpredictability, Adonis shields his head while doing his best to ignore their shrill calls. They continue to circle faster and with more aggression.

Hearing their persistent squawks, he cannot help but think they have been sent to convey a message meant for him. Finally, unable to fully contain his curiosity, he peeks to look.

As his head lifts, one seagull swoops low enough to graze the top of his hat. Frantically, he swats at the air to fend it off.

As the bird rhythmically screeches its discontent, it lands near him, perching on the porch railing. Adonis looks directly into its eyes. A mysterious nature emanates from the two beady black orbs. Something about them creates a sense of foreboding, and the prolonged exchange makes him uncomfortable.

As the bird stares deeper into his soul, its head tilts; its tiny eyes warn him that something ominous is coming, urging him to run.

Although he is drawn to inquire from whom and why it is only a bird, asking will not elicit the response he seeks. Pulling his gaze away, he turns and fervently begins pounding on the door. "Come on, just open up and let me in," he says. "I know you and I didn't start on the best foot, but that's all behind us now."

Irritated by the alarm in his voice and still wanting to get his attention, the bird attempts to end his piercing appeal by cawing louder.

Adonis tries to shut the noise out, but the enraging disturbance persists. Each high-pitched shriek makes him wince; he cannot focus. His shoulders raise to his ears to muffle the sound as he talks louder. "I know a lot has happened. I mean... you...you chained me to the bed and... I won't ask where my clothes went, man. That's your business, not mine."

The frantic nature of his tone sends an alarm to the birds circling above, and in unison, they swoop, grazing the murky water with their clawed, webbed feet. The chaos resonates like a battle ensuing behind him, further cluttering his thoughts.

Tightly shutting his eyes, he pinches the skin of his forehead with trembling fingers as he focuses on the splashing water and tries to overcome the feeling that he is being irrational.

He worries the mayhem is causing him to lose ground with his captor, and his anxiety instigates him to talk louder and faster. "I'll tell you what. I feel like that's all behind us." Then, placing his palms against the door, he leans his head closer. "If you let me inside right now, and I mean right now, I swear on my momma's grave, I won't ask a single question about anything that has happened here. Everyone has their quirks. God only knows I have some myself."

His eyes dart from left to right. Sweat drips from his forehead and blurs his vision. He cannot take the anticipation of waiting for the clicking sound of the door's latch much longer.

Feeding off the booming resonance of his pounding heartbeats, the birds' heckling amplifies. Their calls consume his mind; He cannot decipher the direction of each caw or clack of their pointed beaks. The emotional confusion turns his mind to slop, and his ability to focus vanishes. Shutting his eyes, he tries to control his hysteria, resting his head against the door's wood. "Come on, help me out. I don't pray much, but I swear, I'll try harder if you let me off this time. I'm not ready to go, especially like this. I'm not done living yet. Give me a chance."

The bird perched on the railing releases a shriek that rises above the rest. Adonis skittishly jumps; something about the noise strikes a nerve in him. It has an odd familiarity that takes him back to his childhood. Uneasy about revisiting that difficult time, his adrenaline ramps up, and his sanity crumbles as he fights to keep hold of his emotional blockages.

He pounds harder on the door for help and, not getting the desired result, stops to take a deep breath to calm his shivering body. Escape is the only thing on his mind as he shouts at the top of his lungs one last time, desperate to make whoever's inside listen to him. "Look, there's some wild shit happening out here! I got to get inside. Now!"

The commotion of the flapping birds' wings stirs louder behind him; they are on a mission. One by one, they propel themselves from the sky, skimming the water before circling the porch, creating a flurry of wind, feathers, and swamp mist.

The whooshing grazes the back of his neck, bringing him to the point of tears as their proximity creates terror inside him. Their impenetrable commotion borders on aggressive; there are more birds than before.

He cannot stand the thought of their piercing little eyes and snapping beaks. The sheer notion of them causes his body to seize. Avoiding turning around, he helplessly whacks on the door one last time, but to no avail. His imagination takes hold as the birds' judgmental glares fixate on him as if they intend to devour his flesh.

The moment evokes several traumatic experiences with birds for Adonis, one of which he experienced during childhood and others while homeless.

Countless times, he woke up on the street after bingeing on substances, only to discover birds pecking at his clothes and skin, feeding on his vomit. Adonis is terrified of the thought of waking up to his face being stripped of its flesh by birds, causing him to cover his head when sleeping outside.

Although there are various reasons he can list for his phobia, a particular one has stuck with him, haunting him daily. It involves one of the few memories he has regarding a parental figure.

From the time he was a baby, his mother had told him that his father's absence was due to his incarceration for possession of weed. Because he was not present, his mother said she was forced to become the sole provider for their household.

Regardless of never knowing the man, Adonis maintained respect for his father. He believed he only did what he needed to support his family, but his mother's opinion differed; she grew spiteful over what she deemed his abandonment. She loathed the burden he'd left her, so much so that she never spoke his name, taking his identity to the grave.

Adonis felt her hatred for men, including him, worsening the older he got.

Men she referred to as boyfriends often came in and out of their lives, making their home feel unsafe. No matter the time of day, she gave them her undivided attention when they visited, kicking him outside to play. His only way of gauging time was by the sun's location in the sky and the varying calls of birds.

It was not until later that he learned that his mother had been working the streets, selling her body to pay for the roof over their head and her addictions. With each man's visit, a piece of her was lost, numbing her heart and turning her cold. She blamed her unhappiness on her life as a single parent and the existence of her young son. By the time he turned three, her lips no longer displayed a smile, and the simple pleasure of humming along to the radio had vanished.

There is a particular day he will never forget. It was a Friday in August, during the summer leading up to his third-grade year. He sat patiently on the concrete slab in front of the house like he had done many times before, eagerly awaiting to hear his mother's call to return indoors once her guest vacated. The day seemed like any other—sitting, counting birds, and listening to the shifting tone of their calls to keep track of the time.

A drop of water landing on his skin confused him; it was not supposed to rain that day. Curious, he took his focus from the birds and looked to the sky to investigate. He found the once-blue sky ominously dark, foretelling an impending storm. The birds, startled by the sudden weather shift, flapped their wings in a frenzy as they swarmed past him, so close that their feathers and feet brushed his skin. They formed a swirling swarm above, crying out in distress, their voices echoing through the air as they turned their backs and flew away, abandoning him.

Even when the rain turned to a downpour, he stayed obedient, waiting for hours in his soaked jeans and t-shirt, only shifting his position once to curl up by the door and sleep. His mother never came to get him, even after the sun rose the following day and the rain finally stopped.

Shivering, he pounded on the door, begging to be let inside; she did not answer. Adonis was sure she had permanently discarded him for a man, leaving him alone as he helplessly slept on the porch with no shelter or hope.

He was only eight years old. Since he had no other family, he knew that he could only rely on himself from then on.

That day marked his first experience with homelessness.

For his first few days alone, he took shelter in an abandoned doghouse, hidden in the weeds of their overgrown backyard, and wandered the streets at night, searching dumpsters for food. After a week passed, he tried one last time to enter their home, but things remained unchanged. Met with the same silence as before, he came to terms with the fact that you cannot make someone love you. He knew she had resented her life being his mother; she'd reminded him daily, so he assumed she'd had enough and ran away, leaving him behind.

On the eighth day of his abandonment, a state police officer who had responded to a car accident on the outskirts of town discovered him rummaging through a dumpster behind the community's only 24-hour diner. Everyone was shocked when he was found alone; they had all presumed he left the town with his mother. He was immediately placed under state custody with no other family of record.

It was not until a month after her disappearance that they discovered a few of her items washed up on the bank of the bayou. Neither she nor her remains were ever found, and minimal attempts were made to locate her or investigate her vanishing, given her line of work.

Her disappearance remained a mystery.

Of course, many developed their own opinion in the small town; some said she ran away with a man, while others claimed she was the victim of a much darker narrative.

Regardless of the rumors or trauma he endured, Adonis could not forget about her. Even as he bounced between foster care and the streets, she was always on his mind. From the moment his mother abandoned him, he made a conscious choice not to dwell on the memories of their complicated past but rather to focus on the hope that someday she would find it in her heart to return for him.

The birds continue to circle and squawk around him. Each of their calls reminds him of his eight-year-old self, sitting on the concrete porch waiting for his mother; it churns his intestines and makes him nauseous.

They land one at a time, slowly flapping their wings, perching in a line next to one another on the railing. As they continue their screaming chants, their tiny black eyes watch him intently from behind.

Unable to take their suffocating screeches any longer, his nerves cause his mind to swirl. He knows the only way to stop them is by confronting his fear. Taking a deep breath, he clenches his fists and turns to face them. In perfect unison, their heads tilt, and their beaks mock him with clacking laughter.

The unsettling image of them lined up in a row, and gawking sets him into a frenzy; something about their beady eyes pushes him to the edge of a panic attack. He wants to escape and to do that, he knows he must get inside. As he continues to watch them, he refrains from blinking not to draw unwanted attention and, reaching behind himself, lightly knocks on the door.

Mid-knock, the birds fall silent. Thinking it is odd, he follows their lead and freezes.

They are fixated on something in the distance.

A rush of anxiety rolls over his body as he focuses on listening more closely. Whispering breaks the peace, quietly reverberating off the water.

The harder he concentrates, the more his heart races.

Even though the sloshing swamp muffles the words, a pitch emulating a woman's tone and the methodical tempo hauntingly resonate.

His eyes widen in confusion. He had thought he was alone.

The melody echoes again. This time, the sound fans out across the endless bayou.

Unsure of the noise's origin, he scans the horizon to search for a clue and, not seeing anything, nervously calls out. "Hell—hello?"

The voice persists, becoming louder.

In unison, the bird's feet shift on the railing and they turn their bodies toward the sound as if entranced by the melody. Their deliberate movement catches his attention. It becomes apparent they are waiting for something's arrival. Curious, he follows their gaze to where they stare off the boat's bow.

Ripples form in the water as if something is releasing breaths beneath its surface. The tiny air bubbles create a pattern in the swamp's current, mapping the direction of the entity's leisurely movement.

It is heading toward the houseboat.

He is terrified by the sight of something swimming toward him. Quickly, he attempts to analyze the shape. His stomach churns at the thought of what horrific creature could lurk beneath the murky water's surface. Little by little, the intruding entity creeps closer from the cypress grove's edge, bringing with it an impenetrable fog that harbors a somber tone.

A haunting voice echoes across the abyss. "Adonis. Adonis," it says.

He freezes; the disturbing cries trigger his pupils to dilate and his skin to turn clammy. "How does it know my name?" he asks; terror plagues his whisper.

Even though the song has an enchanting quality, he finds it disturbing; within it lies an odd air of hostility. There is an unidentifiable evil that toys with his mind as it playfully dabbles within its call. "No need to be afraid, child," it says with a serpent's lisp.

Each prowling movement in the water petrifies him, quickening his breath. Feeling faint, his legs buckle. He grabs ahold of the house's siding to keep himself from collapsing. He wants to close his eyes to escape but knows it's useless.

Remnants of the breeze cling to his name, continuing to reverberate across the top of the swamp, taunting him. He scans the horizon to see to whom the voice belongs and feels powerless after turning up empty-handed. Overcome by desperation, he tries to call to it. "Who ... who's there?" he asks.

The melody grows louder in reply, each note exuding a gurgling, raspy tone, creating a wave of agony that envelopes him, filling the air with a static that forms tiny goosebumps on the back of his neck. He is held captive by every sliding scale, as if heavy sandbags lay on the tops of his feet, weighing him down.

The haunting noise grows, and his eyes water as they dart toward every echo to pinpoint the origin. He rubs his ears to make the sound stop, believing he may go insane.

As it moves closer, his eyes catch a ripple in the stagnant swamp near the front of the houseboat. He anxiously watches the water pattern, confirming that the voice is coming from the bubbles approaching the porch.

Something is swimming underneath the surface, and it is not an alligator.

His lip quivers over what is lurking. Fighting his terror, he places a palm against the door to stay grounded and leans closer to get a better look.

As the rippling reaches the porch's wooden steps, it stops. The water's sudden stillness is unsettling, triggering him into a downward spiral and slowing the world to a crawl around him.

He glimpses the birds from the corner of his eye. Their feathers ruffle in unison as they remain fixated on the porch's first step. They sense something instinctually alarming, and the prospect of what it could be shallows Adonis's breathing and sends his heart into rapid palpitations.

Although he wants to look away, he cannot. There is an element about the peacefulness of the water that eerily calls to him. No matter his fear, he yearns to know what is hidden beneath its surface.

Movement at the boat's edge breaks through the fleeting tranquility. Adonis trembles with fear as a pair of yellow eyes emerge from the dark abyss. His veins flood with terror as he fixates on the glowing pupils and realizes that the silhouette is a human female, not an animal.

Her stare is relentless; she does not blink.

He is drawn to match her glare. Unable to look away, he squints to get a better view. An unusual emotion surrounds him; even though he knows he should be horrified, he finds something about her leer calming; the eyes have an element of familiarity.

Despite the movement of the water, she remains still, floating. The wind increases, causing small waves to form around her. As she continues staring at him, the swamp foam splashes over the broad bridge of her nose and carries her coiled black locks, fanning them behind her.

He is mesmerized as he watches each strand serenely floating among the ripples; the calm is unsettling.

Her eyes bulge as she analyzes his movements and mannerisms.

Although the evidence is directly in front of him, he cannot process the idea of the thing being human. "You ... you... cannot be real. Only creatures live in the swamp water, not people," he says, stammering as he tries to calm his nerves. "I know that for a fact. Only fish and gators hold their breath that long. A person would die doing that."

The woman remains silent, her eyes locked on him as her withered hand abruptly shoots out of the water.

His mouth gapes open in shock. "What—what the..." he says. Pushing his back into the door, he watches in horror as her skinless digits grab ahold of the deck's bottom step and her blackened nails dig deep into the wood.

He looks for an option to escape, but there is nowhere to go besides the swamp. The mere thought of plunging into alligator-infested water makes him shudder.

The woman's bony knuckles crack as she stretches her hands to the edge of the next step. She pulls herself closer to Adonis, revealing more of her body as she drags herself toward the deck of the houseboat. He fixates on the skin of her arms. Their once beautiful ebony complexion has been wholly replaced with rotted flesh and putrid secretions. The smell of her is reminiscent of rotten chum.

Slowly, her mouth hinges open, and she coughs up a mound of algae-coated moss. Adonis's eyes fill with shock and fixate on the green sludge as it tumbles from her gaping jaw onto the wooden planks.

As she reaches the last step, a raspy groan escapes her lungs.

His gaze locks on the sight of the deteriorating corpse, and, in a panic, he spins around and begins pounding on the cabin door. "Come on, man, you got to let me in," he says, hitting the wood harder. "Dammit, why aren't you listening to me?"

She hears his frantic pleas and stops, leaving her body's lower half concealed in the swamp. With her belly resting on the steps, she shifts her pupils to look up at him; the muscles of her face tense, causing tiny twitches underneath her seedy skin as she forms a smile. "Adonis," she says, "You didn't save me. You didn't even try. After everything I have done for you, you just left me for dead."

Hearing her voice stops him dead in his tracks. He recognizes it as his mother's. "No ... no...It can't be you." He says, shaking his head in disbelief.

She slithers up the rest of the way out of the water and onto the deck, her mouth fixed in an unnerving grin. He watches with horror as her fetid intestines dangle from the jagged opening created by the missing lower half of her body. Then, in a frenzy, he pounds harder against the door. "Come on, man, let me in. Please let me in. I will do anything," he says.

She releases a feral hiss, and her matted curls fall into her face. "This is your fault. You're the reason this happened to me," she says. Her spine contorts to an unnatural arch as her fingers push against the deck and prop what is left of her into an upright position.

Seeing her aggressive look and horrific appearance sends tremors through his body. He shakes uncontrollably, and tears fill his eyes. "It's not my fault. I didn't do a goddamned thing to you!" he yells. Angered by the accusation, he points his finger at her and continues, "You left me outside alone to fend for myself. You abandoned me for some fucking man. You did that shit to yourself."

She drags herself toward him with a fixated stare as her smile leisurely grows to a snarl. The birds follow her motion, shifting their position to face the door. Their nature turns threatening, chaotically squawking and flapping their wings.

Adonis is paralyzed as he watches his mother's mutilated torso crawl toward him. With nowhere to run, he looks again at the boat railing and gulps. He knows there is no other option but to face his fear.

As her grotesque hand reaches for his ankle, he lunges toward the wooden rail while waving his arms to shoo away the birds and make room for him to get out of her reach.

His attempt to escape causes her to move faster with a vengeance. She digs her fingers into the worn floorboards, pulling herself along, continuing her trajectory toward him.

Unwilling to look at her, he sits on the railing, focusing on the water. He buries his eyes in the nook of his elbow while contemplating whether to jump. "I don't deserve this. I'm not a bad guy. I'm far from perfect, but I know damn well I didn't do anything to make you look like that," he says, his emotions boiling over. He hyperventilates as tears fall down his cheeks and snot pools at the base of his nose. "You left me to fend for myself. I was just a kid!"

She replies with a moan.

In a moment of vulnerability, guilt overwhelms him over his outburst. His voice cracks as he wails, "I'm sorry, momma, I swear. I tried to be a good kid. I would have helped you if I could."

All becomes quiet as a beam of sunlight graces his damp cheeks.

The click of the front door unlatching pierces the stagnant air. As a soft breeze brushes his skin, he reluctantly raises his head from his trembling arm to look. Suddenly, he is startled by a loud splash emanating from the swamp; he jumps and quickly turns to face the source. His gaze is met by a solitary bird resting on the railing; then, focusing on the water, he discovers a set of alligator eyes peering back at him. He watches with horror as its jaws open, and, with a lunge and quick snap, it barely misses the perching bird. Upon its failure, the creature's belly slaps the water, creating a loud splash as its body sinks below the murky surface.

The bird remains unfazed by the attack.

Adonis gasps for air, and his heart races as he checks his body for any sign of harm. He scans the swamp, searching for the creature. "Sure as hell not gonna be next," he says, then hops down from the railing onto the wooden deck.

As he struggles to catch his breath, he glances at the front door, considering his next move. It appears more inviting than before.

Although he is ready to curse out whoever has locked him outside, he knows now is not the time to push his luck; he must play his cards right. Shaking off his jitters, he takes a deep breath and steadies himself as he rushes towards the entrance.

The bird cocks its head as it watches him return inside. Surrounded by solitude, it emits a final screech as it flies away, joining its flock in the distance.

Four

DON'T MOVE

A donis bursts into the room, slamming the door behind him, and begins grabbing for the lock while catching his breath. Even though the rusted latch is within inches of his trembling hand, it seems so far away.

As he tries to clear his mind, flashes of the decrepit swamp creature continue haunting him, appearing on the backs of his eyelids with every blink. The terror of the image triggers a wave of anxiety. He does not want her to return.

With a deep exhalation, he tightens his grip on the dead-bolt's frigid metal. He attempts to turn it, but it refuses to budge.

Even as he applies even more force, the object remains stuck.

As he realizes it is already locked, his fingers pause on the metal momentarily, and his complexion turns pallid. There is no emotion on his face, only a blank stare. "Huh ... that's strange," he says.

A loud whisper distracts him as something vies for his attention. The mumbled words send shivers down his spine and ring in his ears. Trying to ignore it, he nervously chuckles. "I must be hearing things."

The noise grows louder, and he can hear it moving toward the kitchen. Suddenly, a cabinet door slams shut, making him jump as if he'd heard a gunshot. It's impossible to ignore, causing his body to tense up in response. "What is wrong with you? You gotta calm down. This isn't the streets. Man, you gotta stay focused." He says, looking back at the door's lock.

The latch is barely discernible under the flickering light of the fixture overhead.

As it catches his attention, he feels a sense of relief. "It's about time someone fixed the lights," he says. Pressure builds between his eyes, and he rubs his temples to relieve it.

Everything remains quiet around him. He shuts his lids to enjoy the moment of peace. His outdoor exposure and the stressful situation have left him tired and eager to put the entire experience behind him and start anew. "I'm sure I must have forgotten that I locked it," he says, his voice laced with uncertainty. "Yeah, that's it. I just forgot, and there's nothing strange about it."

Out of nowhere, whispers emerge from the living room. Despite being spoken softly, the words have a distinct sharpness to them. "Hello, Adonis," they say. "We have been waiting for you... to join us."

The voice shatters his belief in finding peace by starting over, filling him with panic. Convinced it is his captor, he refrains from turning around, his jaw clenched. His nerves cause him to sweat, and, dwelling on each word, he works up the courage to speak.

The hallway floorboards ominously creak as heavy footsteps weigh them down.

He swallows the lump in his throat as he listens closer.

Tiny water droplets trickle to the floor with each step.

His body trembles uncontrollably. To ease the tension, he shouts over his shoulder. "You know, man, I appreciate you." Nervously clearing his throat, he continues. "I have a good feeling about this living situation we got going on. I don't know if you've seen it, but things are pretty rough outside ... we must have gotten undocked or something. I can't quite figure out what is happening out there."

A subtle whisper echoes from the hall.

His speech quickens as the eerie sound intensifies his anxiety. "Well ... Maybe you can fill in the blanks for me later. It's no big deal. No pressure. It shouldn't be long before someone notices the houseboat is gone or we run into land. Either way, all this mess will clear up in no time."

The murmurs cease, and he is left in silence.

He readies himself to confront whoever is lurking behind him. As he turns around, his eyes shift to each corner of the room, but no one is there. The room's emptiness confuses him; he does not know where someone could run off to in the confined space. He raises his voice, hoping to draw them out. "Hey, no need to hide. I'm just glad you let me back in," he says.

As he takes another scan, his attention turns to the kitchen. The surfaces have been cleared and cleaned. He walks over and checks for dust by running his fingertip across the countertop; it is spotless. "I see you've been busy cleaning the place up. I know you're in here somewhere, and this old shack isn't that big, so it's only a matter of time before we cross paths," he says.

The living room fills with the clamor of an individual's flat-footed steps behind him, each producing a loud creak.

"Gotcha," he says with a smirk, spinning around to look.

The room is empty.

Conflicted about where the person could have gone, he frantically checks his surroundings, his eyes darting from one object to another until they finally settle on the window. The fading light filters through the curtains and glass from the outside. He fixates on the fabric's feeble glow; the sky appears darker than he expected. "I know I was not out there for that long," he says.

Wanting a better view, he rushes to the small window and pushes the curtains aside.

The sun gives way to the moon, casting a dark orange shade across the sky.

In disbelief, he rubs his chin. He relinquishes control because he cannot argue with physical proof. "Looks like I was wrong... Guess I lost track of time out there," he says. As he shrugs, he notices a reflection in the glass.

The freshly polished window is backed by the darkness, creating a mirror-like effect, revealing a shadowy man peering back at him.

They exchange a silent gaze, staring each other down. It sends a spine-chilling sensation down his back. He finds the dark form startling.

Despite his uneasiness, he tentatively raises his hand to test the ominous presence. The figure imitates his movements slowly and deliberately, relieving his nerves. "Just my reflection. That's all it is," he says. He lowers his arm, and it follows suit, putting its arm down.

Even though he has confirmed it is his image, he cannot help sensing an element of detachment from the person staring back at him. It triggers his paranoia, and he nervously chuckles to ease the tension.

The dark, faceless figure stays motionless, its gaze cold and lifeless as it stares back at him. He notices the likeness is not laughing with him, and he stops to focus on the silhouette.

A foreboding presence lingers in the atmosphere as faint murmurs permeate the room. The sound grows louder, their hypnotic quality intensifying the building's chaos and creating a sense of anarchy.

The presence entices him. He takes a step closer, drawn in by his curiosity, not realizing the strength of its attraction. The reflection remains still. Even though he cannot see the precise details of its facial expression through the darkness, its aura infiltrates his soul, sending shivers down his spine.

He steps forward and notices that the man's outline remains unchanged. Fear grips him, causing his body to halt and his heart to pound in his chest.

Suddenly, the likeness's head turns to the right before freezing in place.

His stomach churns as he gazes at its profile, scrutinizing every detail. He cannot comprehend how it appears indistinguishable to him yet possesses its own will.

The thought of what the reflection's mysterious stare may be fixated on terrifies him. He does not want to look and attempts to subdue his spiraling thoughts by taking a moment to breathe.

As the whispering voices grow louder around him, they resonate like a pit of writhing snakes. Unable to focus, he slaps his cheek and tries to regain control. "Man up," he says.

The murmurs gain force, increasing in volume.

He notices one voice that stands out among the others. It is the woman from the swamp; her words rise over the top of the rest.

The harsh tone strikes a nerve in him, escalating his panic. With every consonant, her voice resounds like an evil incantation, and her speech causes a significant shift in the room's temperature.

As the air heats, a wave of humidity sweeps the room. It makes his palms clammy and his body uncomfortable. His mind runs in circles, and he cannot focus. He screams at the top of his lungs, desperate for the chaos to end. "Stop! " His voice cracking under the force of his words.

The woman's sharp screech cuts through the air as if mocking his misery. He experiences a sense of helplessness as he listens to the tormented howl seeping through the window's seal. Her tone reverberates from the marsh like the wind's mournful cry to the moon.

"Adonis, it's your time now, my child," she says, her eyes emerging from the water. "Come and join the alligators and myself for a swim."

Two beady, glowing dots catch his attention as he stares through the window and over the swamp. Their unwavering glare fixates on him, and as she draws nearer, his anxiety intensifies. "What do you want from me? Huh? Haven't you done enough to fuck up my life?" he asks.

Her face surfaces and her lips curl into a devious grin, revealing her anticipation, ready to begin the hunt. "They will slash your skin and shake you until every vertebra in your neck fractures and your limbs become numb. But do not worry. All will be relatively painless," she says, her words exuding odd happiness.

He winces and frantically shakes his head. "I'm—I'm not going in there," he says. "No, mamma, you can't make me. Exhibiting signs of exhaustion, his head pounds, and his voice is raspy.

She sings the same melody as before. Each of the haunting notes eats away at his resistance to join her. His deep desire to flee the mental torture only exacerbates his desperation. No matter how hard he tries to block her from his mind, guilt over disappointing her consumes him.

A male's voice cuts through the room's bedlam, gently murmuring in his ear. "Behind you," he says. There is a warmth about it that masks the ominous hiss of the serpent's song outside.

Adonis takes it as an omen that he must move forward. "If you want to get out of here, you got to move," he says, fighting his paralysis. He gives himself a stern lecture, saying,

"Seriously, stop acting like a damn baby. She can't get you."

The sounds of the whispering escalate. Turning around, his legs shake, and his throat tightens. His eyes bulge as he claws at his neck, gasping, his wide eyes filled with terror as he struggles to catch his breath, believing this is the punishment for defying his mother.

Without warning, something thwacks the window. Startled, he jumps, his heart slamming against his chest wall as he completes his pivot toward the source of the noise.

The woman's voice vanishes, along with his torture, leaving only the lingering whispers of the others. Above, the light fixture's bulb dims, casting an eerie ambiance over the space.

Adonis's breaths become shallow and rapid as his eyes dart across the room, hunting for the man he had seen in the glass.

He is nowhere to be found.

Refusing to believe that what he saw was a ghost, he searches for any explanation. Finally, his eyes land on the couch, and he spots a peculiar detail: even though it is empty, the cushion exhibits a deep indentation, as if the weight of a slumped body has taken a seat.

He squints to get a closer look while calling out. "Is someone there?"

A raspy male voice responds, whispering so closely to his ear that he can detect puffs of breath. "Get out!" it says.

Abruptly, the warning stops, and he is left in a state of panic. Unable to move, he stares, paralyzed, facing the sofa.

The voice speaks again, sounding so sharp that it cuts through him like a knife. "He's coming. Run!" It screams.

Adonis is horrified as he realizes that the sound is now emanating from within him. He opens his mouth to speak, but his fear inhibits his ability to form words.

He remains frozen, unable to move, as he watches the couch cushion re-inflate, leaving no doubt that whatever had been sitting is rising to its feet. His internal terror holds him helplessly captive. Tears flood his ducts and overflow his lids as his palms sweat and breaths become shallow.

The indentation is wholly gone.

After a long, torturous moment of pause, heavy, dragging footsteps approach him one by one.

He knows he only has a little time before the presence crosses the room. In a sudden surge of adrenaline, he breaks free from the psychological hold of the ominous figure.

The spectral footsteps come to an abrupt halt.

Despite his lack of a plan, Adonis seizes his opportunity to escape, nearly spinning in circles as he searches for a way out. He glimpses the window and is immediately stopped by the glass's reflection.

The man has returned and is standing behind him. His image is more precise than before, confirming that what he once believed to be his reflection is a separate entity.

Adonis fixates on his doppelgänger's face. A little over half of the features look like him, but the skin around the man's eye droops slightly, making the symmetry uneven.

As he stares at each similar feature, he feels a hot breath tickle the back of his neck, provoking a wave of fear like he has never felt before.

The man does not blink as his mouth stretches into a grin, and he gives a silent chuckle. His tongue slides forward, escaping his toothless gums and pushing a puddle of drool onto his chin.

Adonis is horrified by the creature's independence. Every warm breath it exhales fills the air with the smell of swamp water and rotten fish.

Its mouth twitches, releasing its smile as it gasps for air. As he watches the reflection struggle for oxygen, a sense of dread grips Adonis, fearing that he, too, may suffer a similar fate.

The figure's breathing becomes raspy, its veins bulge, and its face turns purple as it clutches its throat in distress.

In an instant, Adonis's worst fear becomes a reality. His entanglement with the entity results in a reversal of roles, and, like a dog on a leash, he is losing control over his actions. With his windpipe closing, he becomes consumed by desperation and pleads. "What do you want?"

The whispers in the room halt their conversation and merge into one, becoming a resounding voice that rings in his ears. "You!" They scream. "You are what he wants."

His vision blurs and the lack of oxygen causes his thoughts to string together. With time running out, he scrambles to gather his breath to make a last plea. "Come … come on, man. I'll do whatever it takes. Just let me go. I don't want to die." He sobs, his words expelling spit as they trail off into a murmur.

The figure replicates him, spewing saliva and silently mocking his tearful plea.

Adonis is on the verge of suffocation, causing his eyesight to blur as he plunges into the surrounding darkness. In his battle for survival, he focuses on each heartbeat pounding like a thunderstorm in his chest.

Something latches onto his shoulders. As the deadly grip tightens, it sears his skin, and he lets out a blood-curdling scream.

The room becomes silent.

Adonis feels a sense of relief as he breathes deeply, realizing his airway is no longer constricted. As his eyesight returns little by little, he notices the man who was behind him is now gone, and he becomes fixated on his reflection.

He massages his cheeks to ease the tension in his jaw and is reassured that his image in the window now precisely matches his every movement.

The light fixture above him momentarily flickers, emitting a buzzing sound before the bulb dies and the room's primary illumination goes out. He watches as the last bit of sunset vanishes from the sky, leaving the vessel surrounded by darkness.

Trying to keep calm, he focuses on the night sky through the window but cannot help noticing a familiar glow from the corner of his eye. The gas lamp, which is positioned on the corner table behind him, is still shining. The flame appears brighter than before, and its heat seems unusually intense. It dances joyfully as its fire rapidly engulfs the wick.

Beads of sweat drip down his face, and he wipes them away with his shirt, cringing at the pain of the fabric rubbing against his shoulder. "Shit," he says. As the sting lingers, he gently touches the affected area to soothe it.

The pain blankets him in anxiety as he recalls being grabbed on the spot earlier. It validates that everything he had experienced was real.

Just when he thinks he has a moment of reprieve, he senses being watched. The thought of something lurking behind him in the glass's reflection terrifies him as he cautiously turns to face the open room.

The couch is occupied once more, but now the entity is visible.

The figure's presence provokes a tsunami of horror in him, sending his leg muscles into uncontrollable fear-filled spasms. Trying to speak, he stammers. "Hell—hello?"

There is no answer.

The gas lamp's flickering flame highlights the man's features; his eyes are closed.

Assuming he is sleeping, Adonis quietly approaches the man to get a better view and immediately notices his ratty attire. It is identical to the clothing he was wearing when he entered the boathouse. "This must be the motherfucker who took my shit," he says.

He takes a step closer, grabs the lamp from the table, and shines it toward the man's face. Startled, he jumps back and gasps as he observes the man's remarkable likeness to himself.

Despite Adonis's reaction, the figure does not flinch, keeping his eyes closed.

In disbelief, his gaze locks on the man's pallid skin and purplish-blue lips until the overpowering smell of human excrement breaks his concentration. Shielding his nose from the sickening odor, he steps back and stops, noticing a slight movement coming from his partially open lips. "Hey man, are ... are you okay?" he asks.

The man's bottom lip parts a little further.

Adonis waits for a moment, expecting him to speak.

Suddenly, he hears a faint buzzing noise, diverting his focus to the man's ear. As the volume becomes louder, a peculiar glow emerges from the canal, causing the outer ear to adopt an eerie red hue and illuminate the blood vessels. Nervously, he wonders about the cause as a firefly unexpectedly emerges, casting its flickering light.

Adonis shudders at the sight of the insect scurrying from his lobe to his chin. He cannot believe the man remains completely still, making him question if he is even alive.

Despite his urge to flee, he cannot resist staring, fixated on the striking similarity to himself. In disbelief, he questions if it's another trick or, worse yet, a foreshadowing of his future. "That's impossible. That thing is not me!" He says.

Abruptly, the man gasps for breath as firefly larvae emerge from his nostrils, ears, and mouth, expelling bloody larvae from his lungs. In a frenzy, his eyes burst open, and he lets out a piercing wail. "Help! He's going to kill me! " He screams.

Adonis is terrified; not only do their features resemble each other, but the voice hauntingly mimics his own.

With a trembling hand, he swings the lantern toward the figure, warding him away. "Don't you come near me now! Get back!" he says.

With his face invaded by squirming larvae, the man scrambles to stand up, his fingers clawing at his skin in horror. Adonis takes his movement as an advance and swipes the kerosene lamp toward him. "I said, get away. I'm warning you."

The man froths at the mouth, becoming crazed, like an animal bitten by a rabid raccoon. Adonis watches in shock as the once-lifeless corpse takes its first step, falls to the floor, and begins crawling toward him.

In a frenzy, Adonis scans the room for a place to hide and, upon spotting a door in the room's corner, sprints toward it, assuming it must be a closet. Furniture banging echoes behind him as the zombie-like entity wildly flails, crawling faster.

Hearing the grown man's muffled moans closing in, he anxiously grabs for the doorknob, pulls it open, and races inside. Upon entering, he feels the weight of the coats brushing against him as he moves further into the small room and closes the door.

Adonis makes his getaway as the man lets out a blood-curdling screech, the sound resembling that of a demon. The terrifying yell makes him wince as he fumbles in the dark to find the latch to lock the door. A sense of relief washes over him as the lock clicks, soothing his nerves.

As the man bludgeons the opposite side of the door, it does not sound human, shaking the frame.

Adonis scurries into the closet's depths, hiding under the jackets, his eyes wide open in the darkness.

Five

WHAT'S HIDDEN IN THE CLOSET

T he closet quakes with every powerful blow, suggesting the wood may fracture at any moment. With each thud, his chest muscles stiffen, and he curls into a tighter ball, seeking comfort by hugging his knees.

The strikes continue, building on top of one another, creating a tornado of chaos and causing him to hyperventilate.

Everything makes it impossible for him to concentrate, and he cannot control the thoughts of his spiraling mind. His heart pounds with the force of implosion.

Out of nowhere, the battering stops; all that is left is the last of the vibrations lingering in the walls. He does not trust the silence; something about the abrupt change makes him skeptical.

Suddenly, the doorknob jiggles, startling him. "Son of a bitch, it's trying to get inside," he says, his whisper barely leaving his mouth.

The handle's movements are mad with aggression. Its hostile nature sends an icy shiver down his spine. The sound is so jarring that he immediately shields his ears while scooting backward until he hits the wall.

A boisterous laugh echoes from the other side of the door, complimenting the animosity.

The tone irks him; he hates feeling weak. With a fierce scream, he lashes out to stand his ground. "You won't break me! You may think you're tough," he shouts, his voice cracking with emotion, "But let me tell you, I've been through shit that would make your head spin—things that are far worse than this crap!"

The only response is the violent twisting of the doorknob. The sound is growing louder and more intense.

He views the lack of a verbal response as disrespect, causing anger to boil within him. He sarcastically chuckles. "Do you know what they call me on the streets? They call me Scraps." The passion behind his words makes him talk louder, spewing spit.

Suddenly, the knob's movement ceases. Overcome with emotion, he drives his point home. "No matter what God throws my way to test me or how much that unforgiving world chews me up and spits me out, I always come back swinging! I'm a survivor, and nothing you do will change that!" Everything remains quiet.

His eyes dart to the handle, and realizing it has stopped moving, he rests his forehead against his knees and shuts his eyes. "Just breathe," he says. Wiping the sweat from his brow, he uses the moment of peace to calm himself down and, with a sigh, looks up at the entrance.

With no windows in the space or gap beneath the door, not a single glimmer of light enters. There is no way of telling how much time has passed.

Trapped within the confines of the pitch-black box, he feels his sanity slipping away. Like a caged animal, he has been removed from the free world and forced to live in ignorance. With nothing for his eyes to focus on, the lack of stimulation causes him to concentrate on his anxious thoughts, which offer him no peace. "I imagine this must be what solitary confinement feels like," he says, grunting out his frustration.

A piece of clothing hanging from the rack brushes against his back. The movement startles him. He finds the sensation of goosebumps flooding his body emasculating. To hide his vulnerability, he clears his throat, shrugs it off, and hastily stands up. "I'm sure there's a light somewhere," he says, glancing up at the ceiling.

As his hands wave in the air, a long dangling chain tickles the backs of his fingers. Quickly, he clutches it in his grasp and pulls.

With a single *click*, an electrical buzz fills the air, and he welcomes the dim light from a bulb. As the filament warms up, its glow becomes brighter. His accomplishment brings him a feeling of ease. "Piece of cake," he says, rubbing his hands together.

The radiance of the lightbulb emits a cozy ambiance, bouncing off the metal of the hangers. Each glint grabs his attention.

He repositions himself to face the clothes hanging from the rod mounted between the wood-paneled walls.

Engrossed in his investigation, he inspects the first few articles of clothing comprising men's coats. "There has to be some sort of clue about your identity here," he says as he rifles through the satin-lined pockets.

Despite his repeated search attempts, he fails to find anything. He tries again to look around the space, searching for any advantage. "I just need a clue—something to help me understand who I'm dealing with," he says, nodding toward the duster jacket. "But damn. Boy, oh boy, does this guy have style. I got to give him that."

The coat is an extravagant, long-hemmed oversized blazer with patches on the shoulders made of cream-colored snakeskin, matching his loafers.

His eyes light up with excitement as he visualizes how he would look wearing it, and, consumed by the anticipation, he cannot help but try it on. He reaches for the garment, and as he pulls it from the hanger, something sharp pokes his finger. It startles him. "Shit," he grumbles, loosening his grip to look at the wound.

The coat falls to the ground.

He places his finger in his mouth to dull the pain and stares at the pricey item sprawled at his feet. Its alluring quality makes him forget any worry.

The jacket is the only thing on his mind.

Dismissing the pain in his finger, he lowers himself to the floor and inches toward it. "Don't be shy, now...... I'm not gonna hurt you," he says jokingly. His fingers trace the sleeve's surface, carefully examining each fold of the soft suede.

Suddenly, the overhead bulb strobes brighter, and the spark of electricity casts a tiny reflection off the tip of a small metal safety pin hidden, unlatched, on the underside of the jacket's lapel. He smiles. "Well, well, well, what do we have here?" he says, directing his attention to the culprit.

It has been perfectly placed through the coat's red silk lining.

His attention lingers on the pin. It is impaling an item—a small piece of paper. He is intrigued by what it may reveal, and curiosity gets the best of him. His fingers wiggle with excitement as he reaches to grab it. "Come to Papa," he says with a chuckle as he delicately plucks it from the fabric, careful not to damage the coat.

Upon closer examination, the object reveals itself as a dry-cleaning receipt, and there appears to be a contact name written on it.

Having the evidence in hand, he grins from ear to ear as he quietly expresses his excitement. "Ooh-wee," he says.

He removes the pin and places it in his pocket for safe-keeping, then scans the receipt. "Well, hello there! It's nice to meet you, A. G ... Gi... Gi." Each letter of the scribbled handwriting is hard to read; its age has caused the paper to turn yellow and the ink to fade. "I'll just call you A.G. from now on," he says.

Still staring at the name, he smirks. "Can you believe it? Our names both start with an A," he says, moving the paper closer. "We're like two sides of the same coin. You know what that means, don't you? What's yours is mine, plain and simple." His fingers caress the suede leather of the jacket while he scans the rest of the receipt for additional details.

Below the name, there is a sequence of numbers, but like everything else, they are difficult to decipher.

His eyes struggle to read in the poor lighting, fueling his frustration. "This looks like chicken scratch," he says.

"Ah, to hell with it! I won't let that kill my vibe," he says. Then, giving up, he shoves the tiny note into his pocket. Redirecting his attention to the coat, he admires it and gives it a playful, smoldering look. "Now, where were we?" Before he can say another word, he snatches it from the floor, brushes the dust off the sleeves, and pulls it on. The smell of its suede revitalizes him, and he wriggles his shoulders with joy.

Above his head, the jacket's lonely hanger sways back and forth without provocation. Its friction against the rod makes an eerie scratching sound, altering the closet's quiet.

Adonis spots the movement out of the corner of his eye and freezes, his fingers still lingering on his lapel. Something about the unprovoked action feels off, sparking his paranoia and sending a frigid chill down his spine. He looks around the space and says, "There's gotta be a vent around here somewhere."

The hanger continues to sway.

Fed up with the incessant movement, he reaches out to stop it, but right before his fingertips make contact, the object comes to a standstill.

Puzzled, he watches it for a moment. "That's strange," he says, jerking his hand away. He shimmies his shoulders to ward off overthinking, then turns to the rack to size up the remaining jackets, only to discover something unexpected.

Rather than posh men's attire, the abutting hanger displays a long brown dress modestly cut and draped elegantly with white eyelet lace. The high neckline is fashioned from a color-coordinated white cable knit. He inspects the garment. "This place just keeps getting more interesting, huh?" he says, pulling the dress toward him.

His eyes flash to the next article of clothing. It is another dress, but it is of a different size and style; the material is ruffled and brightly colored. The high neckline and traditionally cut hems are the only commonality between them.

One after the next, he thumbs through the hangers and chuckles. "Man, this guy is full of surprises."

The remaining rack is filled with more women's dresses, and the various sizes and colors make it clear that they do not belong to the same person. Despite their significant differences, all possess two distinctive characteristics—a high neckline and a modest skirt.

Reaching the last hanging item, he stops and shakes his head in disbelief. "There must be nearly twenty here. I gotta say, either the guy's hiding something, or he's luckier with women than I thought," he says, scanning the dresses again. For a moment, he imagines being the man with so many ladies interested in him. "Damn, I wish I had that game," he says.

The room's silence aids his fantasy.

As an idea occurs to him, his gaze moves to the lapel of his jacket, and with a sense of satisfaction, he pivots on his heels to face the adjacent wall. "Watch out, ladies."

He chuckles. "Ooh-wee, I am fine as wine." Staring at the blank wall, he tunes out his surroundings and, pretending a floor-length mirror exists, poses to display his charm. "How can you resist?" He says, imagining a group of women lining up to have their shot with him.

While preparing for his imaginary conquests, he becomes complacent about his surroundings and the growing darkness lurking near the clothing. Without making a sound, the brown skirt of the closest dress on the rack slowly lifts, and the material turns ever so slightly as if someone is intently examining its eyelet details.

Caught up in his fantasy, he playfully removes his hat to greet the first woman in line. Then, pulling an imaginary brush from the inside pocket of his jacket, he licks his teeth while pretending to run the boar bristles over his short hair. "That sounds pretty far out, but as you can see, I'm a busy man," he says, winking. "But hey, maybe if you are lucky, I'll have some time next week for a little romance. You know us busy men are in high demand. "

The white eyelet lace returns to its original position, but a stirring presence persists beneath the skirt. Abruptly, a pair of beige stockings gradually unravels from the waist and extends beyond the dress's hemline. The thick material lifelessly hangs for a moment before slowly inflating to take the shape of a woman's slender legs.

Still facing the wall, Adonis takes the hat off his head and pops the collar of his dress shirt while continuing his one-sided conversation. "I don't know what to tell you, babe. I'm a cool cat. It's both a blessing and a curse being this fly. I wish there were more time in the day so I could hang out with every fallen angel, just like you, my sweet thing,"

Behind him, the legs of the nylons have already fully manifested into feet, calves, and thighs; each toe wiggles as one-foot stretches. The dress's bodice follows, inflating, the ribcage bloating with a heap of lifeless organs. As the dress's long sleeves expand, they take shape with joints, muscles, and skin. Newly sprouted fingers flex and twist into fists.

As dark caramel skin pushes through the neck-hole of the light brown cotton, a featureless face is revealed. Curly strands of hair stick out from the blank canvas like a pincushion. Slowly, they shift, advancing to the back of the skull's clay-like flesh to take their rightful place, crafting a hairline. The facial characteristics of a woman pulsate beneath a thin translucent membrane layer woven with nerves and veins. The skin is stretched so tightly that it gives the appearance of suffocating the face that lies beneath it.

Adonis confidently flips his hat into the air, concentrating solely on the wall ahead as he nonchalantly expects it to land back on his head.

The brim spins like a bowl as it hits the floor behind him. As the hat rolls away, his face flushes with embarrassment. "No need to fret, ladies. It's part of the show," he says. He scrambles to the ground, crawling on his hands and knees to find where it landed.

The felt edge barely peeks out from beneath the rack of clothes.

Concentrating on redeeming himself, his attention shifts to retrieving the item. "Come to Papa," he says as he extends his arm to fetch it.

Suddenly, the fedora vanishes, sucked deeper into the closet. Surprised by the swift movement, Adonis freezes mid-crawl. He stares at the empty spot where it once was, feeling confused over how he did not see the hand that grabbed it. He drops to his stomach. Keeping a cautious distance, he eyes the space beneath the row of dresses. "Where did you go?" he asks.

He notices something dangling above him, swaying ever so slightly. Despite glimpsing the movement in his peripheral vision, he disregards the distraction and steadfastly focuses on finding the hat. He scans the area again, crawling closer for a better look.

As he inhales, he feels a burning sensation from a potent odor in his nostrils. The stench is something he recognized all too well, having spent countless nights in alleys and rummaging through dumpsters for food.

It is the scent of decay and the sickly-sweet reek of rotten meat.

The repulsive odor lingers under his nose, causing his body to shake uncontrollably with memories of his past. His throat constricts in a dry heave, and as he opens his eyes, he is horrified to see a toe wriggling in front of him.

He scurries backward in a frenzied panic, and upon gaining a clearer view, he sees the pair of calves dangling beneath the brown dress. Their swinging motion is almost hypnotic, drawing him in. Unable to look away, his eyes follow their subtle movement. In a rhythmic pattern, they continue to swing, and the body's heaviness against the hanger causes the metal to scratch the rod, creating an ear-burning screech ... screech...screech.

The sound puts goosebumps on his skin. He wants to cover his ears, but his fear petrifies him, gluing his hands to the floor. As his body trembles, his muscles ache. He tries to speak, but his words are trapped in his throat, refusing to leave his mouth. "That ... that... that's," he finally says, his eyes locked in an unwavering stare on the dangling appendages. Sweat rolls down his forehead. Flustered, he tries again to speak. "Holy shit ... those are damn feet." His chest tightens as his stress levels rise like a pressure cooker about to burst. With his mouth agape, his eyes slowly scan her body.

The bones of the protruding ankles crack as the arches of the feet flex. A high-pitched shriek sounds near the top of the hanger, resembling the cry of a dying animal.

A wave of terror runs through his veins, turning his skin clammy and cold. Fearful of confronting what made the noise, he gulps and cannot bring himself to look beyond her waist.

Again, an ear-shattering shrill echoes above his head, but it's much clearer this time. The unsettling pitch and tone of the scream leave no doubt that it is a woman in distress. As the bloodcurdling call hauntingly resonates between the closely set walls, it creates an echo, smearing each bellow into the next.

Every shrill note causes him to wince, sending an icy shiver down his spine. Dwelling on his anxious thoughts triggers a fit of hyperventilation. Quickly, he shuts his eyes and tries to clear his head. "My mind's gotta be playing tricks on me. No way this is real. I checked those dresses out, and there was nothing in them. Nothing. Swear on my life, those dresses were empty before," he says, tears of desperation forming in his eyes. "Come on, snap out of it. Get your act together, man." He says as he tries to regain control.

Abruptly, the woman inhales a loud, raspy breath.

The disturbing noise strikes a nerve, and his eyes spring open, yet he can't muster the courage to look directly at what is causing it.

With each fraught inhale and exhale, the skin covering her face expands and retracts. Its translucent sheen resembles someone blowing a bubble from chewing gum. Inhaling sharply, she struggles to breathe as the covering gets pulled into her throat. The obstruction causes her to choke, and her heavy coughs spew wet specks of green debris, spattering the translucent vascular shield.

Adonis scrambles to his knees while covering his ears. He mutters as he tries to build the courage to face what is before him. "You gotta face your fears, man; nothing is that bad," he says.

Her screams grow louder.

With a nervous shrug, drops of sweat cascade down his forehead and drip to the floor. "Sounds like the devils got her, but what would you expect? Everything around here is whack; this is nothing. I've faced worse living on the street. Now, I gotta say that sea creature ... that was some scary shit! This is no big deal," he says.

Filled with a surge of confidence, he looks up. "Mother-fuck..."

He is shocked by what he sees, stopping his speech mid-thought. Squinching his eyes shut, he tries giving himself a pep talk, but as soon as he re-opens his lids, the green gunk-covered membrane flexing in and out grabs his attention. "Oh, shit," he says, taking another look; the sight of her is worse than he expected, and he panics.

Her hazy eyes linger on him as she continues to gasp for air. Nervously shifting his gawp, he cannot help noticing how the dress perfectly fits her frail frame; it is like it was made for her.

Her moist, guttural cough reverberates loudly through the confined room. The disturbing sound drags his gaze back to her face; again, her unsettling condition triggers anxiety. He attempts to appear unbothered, but the repulsive view sends waves of nausea through his body, resulting in his stomach violently dry heaving.

Her muffled pleas trigger the lights to flicker as she suffocates and desperately kicks the air, trying to find the floor.

Though terrifying, everything about the situation confuses him and oddly pulls at his empathy. He cannot stand watching her suffer. "Do ... do you need help? Blink once if you do and twice if you don't," he says under his breath.

Her flailing worsens.

Still contemplating, he fidgets; her jarring motions are unnerving. He scrambles to his feet, his mind racing as he tries to figure out what to do next.

The light strobes faster overhead, mirroring her distress.

Caught in the moral turpitude of guilt, his heart races. Time has run out for him to decide, and he watches as her movements precipitously stop. The weight of her skull becomes heavy on her fragile neck, and it limply hangs forward.

Simultaneously, the light bulb stops flickering, returning to a dimmer glow than before; everything appears calm.

Wiping the nervous sweat from his forehead, he watches her, unsure of what he has just witnessed.

She appears at peace.

Even though he cannot spot any lingering signs of life, he refuses to let his intuition guide him, and, keeping at an arm's length away; his eyes drift to her chest for clues of breath. "Miss?" he asks; his worry prompts a steady quiver in his voice.

She remains perfectly still, not even a muscle twitching.

The soft lighting from above evenly dusts the back of her hunching neck. As it trickles onto the nape, it highlights a short row of protruding vertebrae, fashioning a map of her bony spine. Its delicate nature is alluring and captures his attention.

As if hypnotized by the tiny section of her spine emerging from her turtleneck, he cautiously steps toward her. "Miss," he says, "are—are you..." Taking a moment of pause, he becomes distracted, trying to place the delicate vertebrae's familiarity.

The weight of her limply hanging head pulls the skin tighter over the ridges of bone.

Just as he is about to correlate the image with memory, he stops, sensing a knot in his throat. "No," he says. "You're not real." Looking at her hair, he gulps and, taking another step, moves his attention back to her neck. He cannot help fixating on the sharp edges of the bones beneath her ashen skin.

Her bare flesh glistens, almost sparkling, like glitter under the soft light.

His sense of unease grows as he observes the woman's skeletal appearance, her frail frame stirring emotions linked to a memory of his early years of homelessness. A wave of sadness runs through him, making him fidget. "No," he says. Not wanting to face his heavy sentiment, he looks to the ground to escape, but his mind will not comply.

The wooden floorboards creak under his feet as he tries to distract himself by twisting his toe against a large knot in one of its planks.

Despite his efforts to refocus his thoughts, his mind wanders further and further toward the memory. His heart races, and his nostrils flare as he takes a deep breath to calm himself.

Out of nowhere, he notices a scent wafting through the air.

He recognizes something about it; he has smelled it before. It is the smell of her skin.

Flustered, he attempts to hold his breath, but it is all he can think about. He cannot sort out his thoughts; the more he fights to subdue his emotions, the more his internal turmoil intensifies.

Without warning, the lightbulb surges, generating an infuriating hum. The additional noise causes his anger to escalate. Ready to snap, he clenches his fists and grunts. "Why are you fucking with me? Huh?" he asks. "Huh?"

As her body sedentarily hangs, her unsettling odor turns rank. The overpowering stench puts him more on edge.

He jumps, convinced that he spots movement from the corner of his eye, but there is none. The silhouette of her figure against the light torments him as he looks at her. He finds her lack of action irking.

The dim lighting emphasizes the coating encasing the strands of her matted hair, giving it a crusty, brittle appearance. Though it makes him uncomfortable, he refuses to look away; he worries about missing any sudden movements.

Mid-stare, the light stops pulsating, settling to a consistent yellow hue and casting an even radiance along her back. The shift in ambiance magnifies his unease, causing his thoughts to become more erratic and his skin to turn a sickly color.

The stagnant air in the room dries out his eyes, forcing him to blink before resuming his paranoid stare. He gasps for air as he fixates on her body, still suspended lifelessly in the same position. Her innocent vulnerability makes it impossible for him to push the memory away any longer.

It was the only time in his life when he thought he had found true love.

He winces at the thought of her. "Cecelia," he says, gasping and shaking his head, his foot nervously tapping the floor. As he works to debunk the irrational idea of the hanging woman being her, he squints with skepticism. Growing increasingly anxious, his speech gains speed. He blurts out, "No ... she's long gone."

Their encounter happened at a time when he still held a glimmer of naivety about the world in his teen years.

He'd felt she was something special from the moment he laid eyes on her. They met while frequenting the same dealer to get their fix, and their connection deepened upon swapping similar stories of abandonment.

Following their first interaction, he knew his life would be forever altered; he was head over heels. She'd ignited in him a belief in love at first sight.

She was the first thing in life that he felt was worth fighting for or living for. Their bond gave him something to look forward to each day and a purpose for waking up each morning. He felt compelled to be a better version of himself because of her.

Even though they both came from tragic upbringings, he felt their emotional connection could overcome the evils that had a hold on them. He made it his mission to protect her from everything, including the detrimental repercussions caused by their struggle with addiction. In his heart, he believed that the power of their connection would give them the strength to stop giving in to their vices.

They agreed to be there for one another. By creating a life together, they would rewrite their narratives for the better and help each other get off the street.

Adonis based his trust on their similarities; he never suspected her of relapsing, let alone lying about her intentions.

It had all unraveled the night before they were supposed to check into a shelter to start their journey together. Living there was supposed to help them get back on their feet. That evening, as the sun set, they held each other close, and he'd felt the impressions of the bones on her lean back. Until then, he had never realized the extent of her skeletal frame; it made him sick thinking of how bad their addictions had become.

Swearing that everything would be better in the morning, he'd closed his eyes, but the night had other plans.

When he'd woken up, she was nowhere to be found.

Her absence had made him frantic; just like his mother, she had abandoned him. Rather than continuing with his plan to check in to the shelter, he allowed her abrupt disappearance to reopen his emotional wounds from his childhood, which he had no intention of facing. For the next couple of years, he made it his mission to search for her, using it as a justification for staying on the streets and maintaining his addiction.

Now, having not thought of her in some time, the image of the limply hanging body draws out emotions he had buried long ago. In his mind, he envisions her corpse on display, and her emaciated state only intensifies the remembrance as every worst-case scenario runs through his mind. "Cece..." he says, scanning her frail frame.

The figure remains motionless as the nickname echoes between the walls.

He shudders; it has been years since those words left his lips. Unable to look away, his mind dissects each similarity to the love of his life, no matter how small. "Why is this happening?" he says, his heart beating rapidly, feeding his dread.

Consumed by grief, he struggles to focus on her profile, his eyelids fluttering as he tries to keep his gaze steady. He finds it impossible to think clearly.

Her hair hangs forward, covering her face. He strains to see her features, but they remain obscured, intensifying his emotions of sadness and anger. Despite being over-whelmed, he wants to move closer and comfort her.

He takes a short step forward until he is within arm's reach and then extends his hand to touch her hair. Nervously, he clears his throat. "Miss? Are ... are you okay?" he asks. Despite not expecting a response, he carefully studies her face, ensuring she does not make any sudden movements that could catch him off-guard.

Finding none, he breathes a sigh of relief.

He is oblivious to her silent eagerness as she waits for him to draw nearer. Little does he know that if he looked closer, he would see her fingers twitching with anticipation just out of his view.

He stretches out a solitary finger and gently prods her. The body feels stiff and unyielding, lacking the suppleness of human skin. Her flesh's odd texture and absence of a response elicit laughter from Adonis, who scans the figure with disbelief. "Yo ... this has gotta be a joke. I bet she's not even real," he says, chuckling. "Man, I knew it."

Hidden beneath the hair and the membrane covering her face, her mouth flinches with a devil's smile.

As his hand lingers near her arm, the lightbulb overhead emits a sudden buzz, causing him to startle. In frustration, he rolls his eyes and mutters under his breath. "Yes, siree, this is one sick damn joke?"

A floorboard creaks in the living room.

Immediately, it seizes his attention. Taking a deep breath, he braces his stance. He bellows at the top of his lungs so that anyone outside the closet can hear him say, "Hey, A.G., I know you're out there! If you're listening, I want to let you know I am on to you! This whole dummy thing is a real drag." Stopping to take another look at her, he continues, "You are one sick son of a bitch, you know that? This isn't cool, man."

The buzz from the light fades into the background.

Out of things to say, his attention drifts to the bulb to check that it remains on; giving it a moment, he watches it remain consistently illuminated and sighs in relief.

He glances at the figure and shakes his head, still feeling disgusted at the situation and for having his emotions toyed with. "This place is a real downer," he says. His eyes drift to something colorful that catches his attention on the floor. It is the feather from his long-lost fedora, sticking out from underneath the row of long skirts.

His excitement causes his eyes to widen; he had thought it was long gone. "I knew you would come back to me," he says with a playful smirk. He leans forward to retrieve it while continuing to talk to himself. "At least something is going right around here."

As he shifts his weight to the floor, something stirs above. The woman's hair gradually sways as her hanging head turns to follow his movement.

Already having written her off, he focuses on the only thing he cares about: his hat.

Taking care not to create any sound, the woman raises her stiff hands over her head and grasps the metal pole attached to the hanger around her neck. Her gaze remains unwaveringly fixed on him while he retrieves his prized object, and she slowly frees herself from the wire's grasp.

The hat's luxurious feel between his fingers makes him smile from ear to ear. Clutching the treasure, he backs out from beneath the clothes and brushes off a small dust bunny while continuing to admire it. "How I've missed you, my friend," he says. Resting it on his head, he briefly closes his eyes to revel in the warmth of his skull. "See, right back where you belong," he says.

The light above him flickers, shattering his contentment. He pauses, and he looks at the bulb. "I thought we were past this," he says.

As he glares at it, a sudden burst of blinding light catches him off-guard, forcing him to shield his eyes.

In an instant, the illumination vanishes, and the space is enveloped in darkness.

Unsure of what is happening, he frantically scans the room for an answer. "Shit," he says. "Shit."

In the pitch-black abyss, the woman uses the hum of the lightbulb's last moments to complete her detachment from the rack. With the hanger still anchored in the back of her dress, she plummets to the ground with a resounding *thud*.

The sound of her hitting the wooden floor causes a shiver to run down his spine. "Just my imagination ... that's all it is," he says.

Her hair hangs over her vacant eyes as she lurks in the darkness. Like a cat hunting at night, she uses the obscurity to her advantage. She crawls below the clothing rack with unnaturally jarring movements as she takes refuge while stalking him.

The sound of her scurrying movement startles him. Unable to see anything around him, his frustration mounts, exacerbating his feeling of being trapped. His body goes into fight-or-flight mode as adrenaline floods his system.

A burst of energy courses through his veins, and he readies himself to face whatever comes his way.

He extends his arms to explore the void in front of him, and a wave of relief washes over him as his fingertips graze the soft fabric of the hanging garments. "See? Everything is cool," he says.

Crouched deep behind the clothes, the reanimated carcass huddles like a feral animal, watching him.

Adonis chuckles at himself. Wanting to erase his moment of weakness, he dusts off his pants and casts his gaze toward the ceiling. "All right, one thing at a time," he says. His trembling hand reaches upward, waving to find the chain attached to the lightbulb. The dangling loop brushes against the back of his hand, and wrapping his fingers around it, he optimistically gives a tug.

Rather than cooperating, after the quiet *click*, nothing happens; the light remains off. "That's a pisser," he says, looking at it with frustration.

Determined to turn his luck around, he gives another yank, this time harder—the light bulb flickers, settling to a much dimmer setting than before.

Knowing that the lighting is erratic, he swiftly examines the clothing rack, looking for evidence of the woman's presence. Not discovering her upon initial inspection reassures him. "Well, at least there's something positive," he says, wiping sweat from his brow.

As he makes another pass, nervously searching the hangers, she quietly watches from the level of his ankles below the skirts, the tip of her stocking-covered toe barely poking out.

Adonis cannot fully remember the dress's color, so not seeing any garments filled with a woman's form, he takes the disappearance as evidence that he had imagined things. "Well, looks like there's nothing to see here. It's wild how your mind can fool you," he says. Taking a step away from the rack, he chuckles.

Keeping quiet, the woman stays hidden behind the clothes, intently watching him and anxiously gnawing at the membrane covering her face. Every snap of her needle-like teeth results in bite-sized perforations. Her lipless mouth cracks open slightly as she extends her tongue in search of an opening. She then employs her sharp claws to shred the holes wider, giving her eyes a clearer view.

Still distracted by the wardrobe's secrets, Adonis searches the garments for more clues, taking another shuffle through the hangers. He squints in concentration as he examines each piece of clothing one by one.

She wiggles her jaw in anticipation as he approaches the grouping of dresses she patiently hides behind.

Midway through the garments, his eyes take notice of the clothing labels. "Come on; there has to be a name or something that will tell me more about you," he says.

As he reaches for the next hanger in line, he spots something peculiar: a few scribble marks on the tag. The poor lighting and distance make it difficult for him to read what it says. He pulls the material toward him, hoping to get a better look at the message.

Seizing the moment of his distraction, the woman slowly crawls out from under the clothing.

With the tag in hand, he pulls it closer and peers at the writing. "How is anyone supposed to read this shit?" He says.

She lets out a menacing growl and lunges toward him, seizing his ankles. "You! " She shrieks, her tongue split down the center, giving each word a hiss.

He winces as she tightens her grip, feeling the searing heat of her touch and smelling the stench of singed flesh and hair.

She taunts. "Killer ... killer... killer," she says.

Overwhelmed by the excruciating pain in his ankles, he crumples to the ground while screaming at the top of his lungs in agony.

She smiles, her silent grin resembling a laughing hyena. She refuses to let go, gripping him tightly, while the reek of his blistered skin makes her nostrils flare.

He shrieks louder.

She drags herself from underneath the clothing, using his body as an anchor. Her demeanor seethes with spite; she wants nothing more than to watch him suffer. "You did this. You did this to me," she says. With each word, saliva drips from the detached skin loosely hanging around her mouth.

He watches with horror as she pulls herself from beneath the dresses. "Did ... did what? I didn't do anything to you! I don't even know you," he says, shaking his head. He kicks his legs to get her off him while yelling louder, "Get back!" His hands scramble frantically on the floor as he tries to crawl away.

The more he fights to escape, the stronger her hold on his legs becomes.

As his hands gain traction against the ground, he drags her with him until his back hits the closet wall. He peers from left to right, but there is nowhere to run.

Her eyes fixate on his jacket, and she growls, hoisting herself onto his knees. "Evil," she says, using her bony fingers to claw her way further up his body.

Quickly, he throws his hands in front of himself to block her gnashing teeth from his face. "I'm telling you, you've got the wrong guy. I swear I didn't do anything to you, I swear," he says. Caught up in terror, he can no longer fight back the tears that now run down his cheeks.

Her snarls cause the bulb to pulsate overhead.

Overcome by his emotions, he glances up at the light. "Now's not the time!" he says, snot bubbles popping from his nostrils.

She refuses to let up and overpowers him. He is powerless to stop her as she frenziedly clutches his wrists, yanking his hands away from his face. Her savage noises mirror a crazed beast on the verge of attacking.

The scorching pain caused by her fiery grip makes him wail in agony. "Please, listen to me. I don't know you," he says.

Her stare widens as she makes direct eye contact with him. "You ... It's you!" she screams.

Suddenly, the lightbulb hums, and the room goes black once again.

Still feeling the weight of her body on him, he knows he cannot hold her off much longer and panics. "Get off me, damn it! " He shouts. With an explosive burst of energy, he shoves her off and breaks free.

As she hits the opposite side of the closet, crashing into the wall, her body emits a horrific crack reminiscent of breaking bones.

Terrified, the sound causes him to tremble as he springs to his feet. His heart racing, he lunges toward the door, his fingers fumbling over the smooth surface, searching for the handle. As he grasps the metallic knob, he foregoes any attempt to unlock it and, exuding force, tears it open. The brute energy rips it from its hinges.

Sprinting for dear life, he races into the center of the living room to escape. As he turns around to face the open doorway, a surge of daylight from the window pelts his face. His hand slowly lifts to feel the warmth on his flushed cheek.

He keeps his distance from the closet, his heart pounding in his chest while he tries to process what happened. As the sunlight filters into the doorless space, it illuminates the spot where he had flung the corpse.

In her place is an assortment of clothes, all still with hangers attached, piled up on the closet floor.

Six

DAYLIGHT WON'T SAVE YOU

Shocked, he shifts his eyes to the doorless room. "What just went down?" he asks. Trying to catch his breath, he stares dumbfounded at the large wooden door.

It is lying on the floor, next to the wall; all the edges have been splintered from the brunt force of its removal.

He had not thought he was strong enough, even with adrenaline, to accomplish such a feat. In shock, he glances at his hands. "Right on," he says while clenching his fists.

Dots of light speckle the floor near his feet, creating an illuminated pathway leading to the closet. Wheezing from exertion, he strives to regain his composure through slow, steady breaths before summoning his bravery. "All right, where is she? I'm ready," he says. With a newfound confidence, he lifts his head and follows the trail of lights to where she was last seen.

The living room is bright with daylight, casting a spotlight on a pile of clothes in the closet. The hangers are still attached, but the garments look as if they have been pulled off in a hurry, creating a mess.

His heart drops to the pit of his stomach. "But... but she... she was just..." he says, his words trailing off in confusion.

The woman who tormented him is nowhere to be found, with only a pile of clothes in her place.

Feeling like he is going crazy, he takes a moment and buries his head in his hands; releasing his frustration, he lets out a muffled scream. "This has gotta be hell," he says. "You know that? This is some nightmare shit." He winces as he speaks, feeling the pain in his burned wrists triggered by the puffs of air escaping his lips.

The chirping birds outside become louder. Their cheerful melody only adds to his irritation as he closes his eyes to concentrate on managing the throbbing burn.

They continue to sing. Unable to take the grating noise, he winces from the pain and swiftly grabs his jacket, using its sleeves to apply pressure to the wounded area. "Jesus Christ, man," he says. His voice cracks as he becomes unhinged and screams at the top of his lungs, "Shut the hell up!"

The birds squawk louder as if to mock him. Anger surges through his veins. The weight of everything that has happened on the houseboat finally becomes too much for him to bear, and he snaps. He aimlessly paces in circles while scanning the room. "Hey! A.G. or whatever the hell your name is. It's time to show yourself!" he shouts. His voice rings so loudly that the effort turns his face red. Continuing his rant, he summons him again, saying, "This shit is getting old, pussy."

Pausing momentarily, he listens for any sound that might indicate his captor's presence while scanning the room for clues. "I know you're in here somewhere. When I was in that closet, I heard the floorboard creak. You can't fool me," he says, his grin twisting to the look of a maniac as his pupils dilate. Then, amid his escalating emotional breakdown, he notices something.

Everything in the living room now exhibits the same level of cleanliness as the kitchen. The place has undergone a complete reset. Convinced he is being messed with, Adonis tenses his jaw and grits his teeth. "He must think I'm some kind of fool," he says. With growing irritation, he does one last scan of his surroundings.

The only disorganized area remaining is the closet, with its broken door, which he ripped off from the hinges.

While the birds outside annoyingly chirp, he wipes the sweat from his forehead and flaps his armpits due to the oppressive humidity. Fed up, he paces the area. "Where are you hiding?" he asks. "Huh? You think you are tough?" Each of his stomps rattles the floorboards.

His footsteps echo through the space without a single reply. The idea of seclusion in his thoughts deepens his downward spiral. "I know I'm not imagining this shit," he says. His anger causes him to grunt as he neurotically scans the room. He cannot take it anymore and plants himself near the window, hoping to distract his thoughts with the view outside.

The blue sky appears normal, filled with scattered clouds resembling cotton puffs, but there's still no sign of land.

As he sees his reflection in the glass, he notices a semi-transparent silhouette of a man smiling behind him. Its presence fills him with rage.

With a stern point toward the window, he seizes the opportunity to unload his frustrations. He wants to make sure the listener is paying attention before he loses them, so he blurts, "There were two ways to do this—the easy or the hard way. I would've given you the choice, but you've already made it. You are a coward. Yeah, that's right. Let me lay that on you again. You are nothing but a Goddamn coward. Hiding won't help. I will hunt you down, and when I find you ... boy oh boy. Get ready to pay for all the shit you've done to me. You know what they say... an eye for an eye. I tried to be cool, but that ship has sailed. I'm done with playing games."

With his attention fixed on the window, he watches the iridescent figure and angrily lifts and drops the corner of the couch. The forceful impact of the sofa hitting the ground leaves deep marks on the floor. "What do you think about that? Huh? I'm just getting started. That's just a little taste of what'll go down if you keep pulling this bullshit! "

Adonis continues. "And by the way, that whole leaving me in the bed butt-ass naked thing was weird, so I'm keeping the outfit. "

He releases an enormous sigh, feeling powerful and in control for the first time. The figure maintains a deadpan expression, never wavering as it remains motionless, watching him intently.

Ready to drive his threat home, Adonis laughs at the sight and, puffing out his chest to show his dominance, shouts louder, pointing to the scuffed floor. "You see that? I'm done playing nice. I'm about to fuck your shit up, so you won't be able to do this whole little clean-up act you've been doing to mess with me. You see, I have nothing to lose, and you have everything. I swear, you're gonna pay for your sick games. I swear on my grave you'll pay!"

Catching his breath from his rant, he expects to see the cowardly man slumped, crumbling into a shell of a person. But instead, without warning, the entity swivels around and sprints away.

Adonis tracks his movement in the window, and his eyes widen. "Oh, hell no, you little weasel," he says, spinning around and searching the room for the culprit.

Suddenly, a loud crash fills the kitchen as one of the cabinet drawers falls to the ground, scattering its contents in all directions. It causes his heart to race, and, hyperventilating, he frantically scans the room, looking for the mysterious man.

He is nowhere in sight; he has vanished.

"How..." he says to himself. Darting toward the kitchen, he yells, "I will find you! I promise you that!"

Left alone, he is met with only an echo of his voice bouncing between the room's walls as he shouts in frustration. As he listens to the stillness, it prompts his spiraling thoughts to worsen. Everything is too quiet.

He scans the area of the spilled drawer, his eyes flinching from side to side. "Well, A.G., if you wanna play this game,

I'm ready. Once I finally escape this dump, you better believe I'm gonna tell everybody I know about this crazy shit. Time to find some more dirt," he mutters, trying to calm down and devise a plan as he heads toward the mess.

Scattered everywhere is an assortment of what appears to be a collection of obscure knickknacks and trinkets of different sorts. He is intrigued; he had been expecting only to see silverware. His eyes dart from one item to the next, gravitating to anything brightly colored. "There's gotta be something here that'll give me the lowdown on you," he says, rubbing his hands together.

He quickly glances at the items before leisurely bending over to investigate. Overwhelmed with where to start, his eyes drift to the edges of a torn picture. Beside it is a jumbled assortment of toothpicks and a small pack of matches. "So, that's where you've been hiding," he says, as his attention is pulled to the small rectangular box. Swiftly picking it up, he holds it to his ear and shakes it to see if anything is left inside. Chuckling, he adds, "Could've used your help earlier."

Even though it does not make much noise, the subtle rattling of the wood lets him know there is at least one match left in the burgundy carton.

He feels he has hit the jackpot. "You know what they say, finders keepers. You can never have too many of these. Never know when you'll need a light," he says, holding up the treasure.

A smile spreads across his face as he excitedly flips the box over to examine each side with curiosity. "Yes sir, you will come in real handy with this broke-ass lighting." He continues analyzing it while talking to himself. Then, delicately sliding the box open, he peers inside, spots the tiny stick's red tip, and chuckles. " You know, growing up, this was all we had at my mamma's place. No candles, just some matches to give light, and you, little guys, always got the job done."

Printed on the front of the container is a name written in cursive, but fading over time has made it illegible. Next to it is a picture of a tiny fish that appears to be a business logo.

He carefully shuts the box, but as he prepares to put it in his coat pocket, the image stops him. "I know that little fish from somewhere," he says. Pondering, he takes another look at the peculiar box's design. "I feel like it's right on the tip of my tongue. Where have I seen it before?" Working to prompt his memory, he flips it over to analyze the back.

There is a scarcely legible telephone number etched into the cardboard. Despite the imprinted marks left by the pen, the ink is smudged, blurring the numbers. "What's up with him and the ladies?" he says, shaking his head and flipping the box over. Again, he looks at the cartoonish depiction of a fish on the front, trying to jog his memory.

Suddenly, his eyes widen with recognition, and he excitedly says, "Oh boy! I know where I've seen you before!" Flicking the logo, he feels satisfied, knowing he has finally solved the mystery. "You came from that nice little fish house ... the one down the street from my childhood home."

Holding the box closer triggers a recollection of one of his few good memories growing up. Before his mother began working the streets, she tried holding a nine-to-five job, wearing a uniform with the same logo. The only reason the image has stuck with him is that on nights she worked, she would bring home scraps for them to eat, and since it was one of the few times he got a full meal, he'd associated the logo with getting fed. "That was some good food. I'll never forget their catfish," he says, salivating. The growling of his stomach drowns out any recollection of her short-lived job despite it being a decent memory.

As he refocuses on the small box in his hand, he notices that the background noise of the birds chirping has died. A mix of emotions floods through him, leaving him feeling conflicted. Though annoying, their squawks provided some company in the silence. Brushing off the thought, Adonis shrugs and refocuses on his investigation.

"What would a man like him be doing in a shit-hole part of town like that? I know if I were him, I wouldn't step foot anywhere over the tracks, especially wearing those get-ups," he says, looking down at his jacket. He puts the matches in his pocket. "None of it makes much sense."

His eyes comb through the mess, and he notices a pattern emerging among the scattered items he had previously overlooked. It comprises more tiny matchboxes, like the one in his pocket. All are dissimilar, each having a different color and design.

His eyes narrow as he concentrates on them. "Huh. Well, I'll be damned ... looks like someone had a hobby," he says. Crawling on his hands and knees, he gathers the small boxes and sets them on the floor in front of him. As with the previous one, they display names of restaurants located across the state of Louisiana.

Sitting on his rear, he analyzes the logos, piecing them together like a puzzle until they form a map of the cities he knows. Each tiny box records the owner's past, painting a story of where he has been in his life's journey.

"Man, got to say ... this cat has been all over the place," he says while studying them for more clues. His nomad lifestyle has proven beneficial, making him proficient at memorizing the lay of the land.

"Huh, that's interesting. There might be more to him than I thought," he says, picking up the boxes. "His things are pretty nice and expensive, but rich folks wouldn't dare go to some places." His fascination grows as he meticulously examines each label, noting the varying degrees of elegance conveyed by the matchboxes of different restaurants. "Must be nice having all that money and eating where you like," he says.

"All right, man, I appreciate your worldly ways, but it's time to shut this party down. I've seen everything I need," he says.

Opening each container, Adonis removes any leftover matchsticks and groups them in the original box inside his jacket pocket. He moves toward the drawer and picks up each item, returning them to where they belong. While handling the matchboxes, he feels the grooves of handwritten phone numbers on their backs and shakes his head.

He whistles a tune as he scans each item and puts them back in their proper place, pausing momentarily to study a black-and-white picture. The photo shows a man roughly the same age as him holding a small child and smiling. In comparison, the child looks petrified, with his eyes wide and pupils dilated, as if a stranger has seized him.

Although the small boy's reaction is odd, Adonis imagines how his life could have been different if he had been that boy. "That kid has no idea how lucky he has it. That's what a proud dad looks like right there," he says, admiring the smiling man.

A surge of emotions overcomes him as he thinks about how he never knew his father. His mother never disclosed the information, nor did she list a name on the birth certificate. It's possible that she was unaware of the specific encounter that resulted in her pregnancy, or she intentionally left it out of the paperwork due to the man's standing in the community or questionable character. Typically, honorable men do not spend their time in the company of prostitutes, so maybe she aimed to protect Adonis from something far worse than simply lacking a father. Whatever the reason, he has no memory of the man.

Clearing his throat, he shifts his gaze to focus on the man in the picture. As he fixates on the minor details, he notices something familiar. "I'd say I recognize that from somewhere." Looking at his lapel, he chuckles. "The man has good taste," he says after noticing that their jackets match. With a smile, he brings the photo closer.

Suddenly, a loud *thud* sounds from the living room, like something has hit the glass.

He flings the photo into the drawer, seizes a wooden spoon, and promptly leaps to his feet. Ready to use the utensil as a weapon, he scans the room. "Who's there?" he asks. While clutching it tightly, he dashes to the doorway and peers into the adjoining space.

It is empty except for the sunlight pouring in.

Shaking out his shoulders, he tries to release his nerves. "Those damn birds are trying to give me a heart attack," he says, returning to the kitchen.

He glances toward the counter and spots the hole where the missing drawer belongs. Without hesitation, he briskly walks toward it. "Ok, easy does it," he says, placing it back in its original spot. He tries closing it, but it stops halfway, refusing to shut. As he pushes harder, he remains oblivious to the small clump of hair that has fallen from the drawer, obstructing the track. With a final shove, it shuts, and he takes a step back to get a better look at the cabinetry. "Those cabinets could use a little oil or something," he says.

Looking at the kitchen makes him yearn for a delicious meal and reminds him of the fish house matchbox in his pocket. His stomach rumbles with hunger. Not remembering the last time he ate, the dull ache consumes his attention. "I'm guessing there's some canned goods or something to eat around here," he says.

The identical drawers left him unsure of which to open first until his eyes were drawn to the large refrigerator at the end of the cabinets. Positioned in the center of its glossy mint-green front are two elongated metal handles, one for the refrigerator compartment and the other for the freezer.

Although he knows the power has had its issues, he is willing to take the gamble on its contents. His reflection on its shiny surface beckons him, calling out his name. "No harm, no foul," he says with a shrug. Walking toward it, he imagines the cold interior blowing chilled air against his skin, and it prickles as goosebumps emerge.

The smudge-free front of the appliance mirrors what he wants to see: a reflection of himself. Slowing his approach, he uses the image to adjust the buttons on his jacket.

Suddenly, a woman's whisper echoes behind him. It summons him by name, triggering the hairs on the back of his neck to stand on end. He is frozen in place as he tries to distract himself from the call by concentrating on the refrigerator.

As the woman's voice lingers, he intently listens to the timbre and recognizes an unsettling familiarity in its tone. The memory of his time in the closet returns, causing his entire body to quiver with an icy sensation. Even though he wants to look, he plants his feet and refrains from turning around. "No way... it can't be Cece," he says, shaking his head in denial. "Nope. No, it's not possible. It's your imagination. She's long gone. We don't need to rehash this; we already went over it. She bugged out a long time ago and is not coming back."

The room's ambiance grows thick with hostility as it fills with the musty scent of damp wood and aged cedar. It has an odor reminiscent of a woodworking shop.

Like a soft breeze, whispers ring through the houseboat's vents, gradually seeping into his mind. As they tear away at his psyche, he shuts his eyes and tries to convince himself it is all in his head. He perspires profusely, fighting to redirect his fear as he listens for surrounding noises—an anxious lump forms in his throat.

Quickly swallowing, he forces his attention to the heavy beats of his heart and releases a sigh. "See? Everything is cool," he says.

A subtle hiss penetrates the space near his ear. Unable to ignore it, his entire body recoils and his knuckles clench. His eyes squeeze shut in panic, accentuating the crow's feet forming above his cheeks.

Silence envelops the room again, and his shoulders relax as he thinks the worst is over.

He is naive to think it is done. Instead, it is waiting, lingering, and closer than before.

His complexion pales as the sounds re-emerge, slowly becoming a complete sentence.

"I'm here, right behind you," the voice says. Its aggression is undeniable and threatening. "Why aren't you looking at me?" Are you rejecting me? "

The voice summons him like a siren to a sailor, eliciting a profound longing that renders him powerless to resist. Losing control of his senses, his vision goes black, and his upper body slowly twists toward the ominous voice. The entity sings a melody that is identical to that of the sea creatures. He is drawn to it like iron to a magnet, and before he knows it, his head is involuntarily turned over halfway to face the voice's direction.

The glint of the sun's reflection off the cabinets catches the corner of his eye, snapping him back to the present and reminding him of his grim situation. He shakes his head to clear his thoughts and redirects his attention back to the sheen of the freezer. Again, his stomach growls. "Now, listen up, Adonis: stay sharp. Look at what's in front of you. Let's just go one step at a time. We gotta eat first before we deal with this other crap! He's looking to break you, " he says, trying to tune everything out. " Since scaring the hell out of me didn't work, he's just gonna let me starve. But no way in hell I'm gonna let that happen."

"Killer," the voice says, shifting from a high-pitched squeal to a menacing growl.

As the laugh resonates behind him, Adonis does his best to convince himself it does not exist; going over and above to prove his point, he releases a boisterous laugh and whistles a merry tune.

The voice continues to taunt him. No longer sounding familiar, it takes on a nonconforming gender, neither female nor male. As its pace quickens, its words take on a sharp, screeching tone. "Run! Get out!" it says. "You better run! Get out before he comes!"

The tone is so gravelly that it's like the shriek of a stone goblin. It causes his eyes to widen and triggers his eardrums to ring. "Leave me alone!" he shouts, his shoulders rising to his ears to shield them from the horrible noise.

The subtle whispers persist and grow louder, filling the room with a chaotic melody of cries. With a grunt, he bolts forward, grips the freezer's metal handle, and, shutting his eyes to focus, prepares to yank the door open.

Abruptly, the room falls silent. The only remaining sounds are his internal deliberations, his pulsating heavy breaths, and the loud beats of his heart. He endeavors to bring his racing thoughts to a halt by closing his eyes and concentrating on the present moment, but his attempts are futile.

His inability to gain even an ounce of control leaves him exasperated, and a single bead of sweat rolling down his nose is the final straw. "Your mind is fucking with you," he says, paralyzed by fear, leaving his hands immobile. One remains on the handle and the other by his side. Licking the sweaty drop from his lips, he clenches his jaw. "That's it—it's all in my mind. None of this exists."

Unsure of his statement, he listens as the room remains abnormally quiet. Although the peace should help his nerves, his mind runs rampant with worry, and his body quivers in fear.

Irritated by his show of weakness, he plows on. Ignoring his emotion, he opens his eyes to look at the freezer. He will take control, ready or not, and his first step is to find food, so he pulls the handle.

An indescribable smell floods his nostrils; it is beyond vile. Trying to connect the scent with a culprit, he quickly scans what is in front of him, but the appliance has no internal light to help guide him, and his body's shadow makes everything darker inside. Although he cannot identify the shelves' contents, he is convinced the freezer has been without power for the better part of a week based on smell alone.

With a slight shift in his stance, he allows the sunlight from the living room to escape around his arms. Gradually, the light brightens the freezer's inside, which is oddly filled with different-sized packages sealed in plastic garbage bags. The items are tightly bound with thick brown shipping tape, and the bags' once deep black color has faded with age.

As he moves closer to get a better look, the putrid odor becomes overpowering. Its gassy reek makes his stomach nauseous, and his intestines churn. "Shit, what did he buy?" he asks himself, fanning the fumes from his face.

His eyes scan the shelves. Trying not to gag, his fingers plug his nostrils to ease the smell. Based on his prior experiences with losing power because of unpaid bills and storms, he is convinced that everything must have been thawed for a week or more before the power turned back on. He digs through the rack closest to him to look for the bag holding the culprit. He concludes he cannot tell what is inside by eyesight alone and uses his free hand to feel the shape of each bag to find anything familiar. A slight layer of frost coats the outside packaging, but the contents feel squishy, confirming his encounters with the houseboats' inconsistent electricity.

His stomach growls in protest, reminding him of how much time has passed and his lack of success in the search. He quickly unloads every item from the upright metal box onto the countertop, intending to open each to see if any hold something edible—preferably a T-Bone steak.

After using his foot to close the door, he hurries toward the row of kitchen cabinets. He opens the first drawer in the line and starts sorting through it. "Come on," he says. "Where are you?" Frustrated after only finding several large rolls of cellophane wrap, he gives up on the first cabinet and moves on to the second.

Its tackiness on the tracks prevents it from opening; no matter how hard he pulls, it does not seem to budge. Frustrated that it is pestering him, rather than giving up and moving on to the next drawer in line, he funnels all his anger into opening it. Despite its resistance, he stubbornly fights back with all his strength, causing his arm muscles to twitch and sweat to bead on his forehead. He grunts at the peak of his anger, and his face turns red. His persistence finally pays off, and it unexpectedly opens, causing him almost to fall backward.

The drawer houses a collection of well-used butcher knives, their blades glistening in the daylight. He looks at them as he catches his breath, the stainless steel reflecting his frazzled face. "That should do the trick," he says, and, not wanting to see how disheveled he is, he quickly grabs the largest one sitting on top and swiftly shuts the drawer.

He pokes his knife into several of the sealed bags, creating small incisions that allow the contents to breathe. The putrid stench flourishes, expanding throughout the kitchen, even more overpowering than before.

An enormous waft hits his nose, and he becomes squeamish, dry heaving as his breaths become shallow. "All this shit must be spoiled," he says, trying to shield his nose. Despite feeling light-headed, he uses a single hand to continue cutting the package's plastic with the most intriguing shape; he wants to see what is inside. Slice by slice, he feels his grip weakening around the knife's handle.

With every cut he makes, another layer of discolored covering is exposed. It irritates him that it is taking so long, and he saws faster. "Does this guy not throw away?" he asks.

Despite his efforts to brave the stench, his throat constricts, and his abdomen contracts to fight back another dry heave. The force of the spasm overtakes him, and his hand clenching the knife slips, causing the blade to penetrate deeply into the bag's contents. The puncture splits the package wide open and produces an unexpected fizzing sound.

He glances at the knife with confusion. "What the hell was that?" He asks.

Slowly, a foul-smelling green foaming liquid oozes from the incision, pooling on the countertop around the bottom of the bags.

Releasing the knife from his grip, he steps back to look at the exposed contents from a different angle, and, seeing what looks like a coiled chunk of human hair, his attention drifts to where the knife has lodged.

The blade is sticking out from the eye socket of a decomposed human head.

Shudders course through his being as his mind analyzes the scene in slow motion. He hyperventilates, his body gasping for air as his fingers anxiously pick at the material of his pants. Gradually, he averts his eyes and scans the other bags. A sense of dread surges within him as he imagines what they might hold—the ominous possibilities cause his heart to descend into the pit of his stomach.

When he thinks back to the other incidents he has encountered, he cannot help concluding that the scene is simply another form of torment by his captor. "Oh, I see what's happening here—he's trying to bring me down. Well, he isn't gonna get that satisfaction. No siree," he says. "I'm nobody's fool, that's for sure."

As the liquid dwindles to its end, a last burst of fizz exits the puncture wound, then stops.

Adonis can visualize the smug look on his captor's face as he observes him like a rat in a lab experiment, and the mere thought of him winning is unbearable. With his fists tightly clenched at his sides, he suppresses the surging waves of rage coursing through his body.

The foul smell lingers in the air, its pungent stench creating an unwanted distraction. Unable to ignore it, his squeamish stomach triggers an influx of acid to migrate up his throat, and he tightens his jaw to keep it down. His muscles shake, and his skin becomes clammy.

There is an abrupt increase in humidity that makes the room even more uncomfortable. While he has mentally determined that everything must be an illusion, the gruesomeness of the scene makes his heart race, and his nerves continue escalating.

Putting on a show to mask his apprehension, he laughs to let the man in charge of the charade know that his attempt to rattle him is ineffective. He clears his throat in preparation to speak. "You know what? I got to give it to you, man—you sure outdid yourself this time," he says. "I don't know how you managed all the theatric shit, but this time, you almost got me."

He waves his finger in the air and, shaking his head, chuckles. "You see, I may not seem like much, but I'm smarter than you think. I'm just letting you know I am on to you, and I can see through all your bullshit."

With each passing moment, the silent room's humidity becomes more oppressive. His leg fidgets beneath him; the image of the decomposed bits of flesh fuels his nausea, and the smell of rot dictates his unease. His jaw clenches as he feels his irritability surge. Determined to stay in control, he snaps his fingers next to his ear to clear his head and regain focus. "Come on, get a hold of yourself," he says. "Don't give him what he wants."

The room's temperature rises, causing an uncomfortable muskiness to settle in the air. The heat messes with his train of thought and drains the saliva from his mouth. Regardless of how much he tries to tell himself everything is okay, his intuition casts doubt on his confidence. A burst of panic fuels his anxiety, and he reluctantly takes a small step forward to get a better glimpse of the remaining bags. "Nice touch," he says, counting them. He nervously tries to make a joke, saying, "I'd say it seems like you got enough bags here to make up a whole damn person."

The plethora of different-shaped wrappings line the countertop; their plastic repels the layer of sludge that seeped from the punctured bag. He scrutinizes the individually wrapped items individually before taking a deep breath. The friction of his dry throat instantly grabs his attention, and he shifts his gaze to the sink at the end of the counter space. He is relieved that the repulsive fluid has yet to migrate into the basin. "Say, I tell you what: I'll put your little art project back where I found it. I just need to get a sip of water first," he says, eyeing the faucet. "You know, if you would quit jacking around the heat, I wouldn't get so damn dehydrated."

Condensation has formed on the surfaces of the bags from the sweltering temperature. Trying to ignore the sight, he avoids eye contact with the gruesome mess and bolts toward the sink. Standing in front of the basin and desperate for relief, he leans forward and reaches for the knob. A gush of liquid bursts from the fixture; the high-pressure spews a mix of stagnant water and rust, creating a pale yellow-brown hue.

The spattering noise makes him freeze, and he can feel the liquid droplets barely missing his lips. "Very funny," he says, keeping his eyes locked on the streaming water while waiting for the color to change. The tin sink vibrates with each burst of water from the faucet, producing a distinctive, tambourine-like ping.

With his back facing the kitchen, he patiently stands by, concentrating on the changing color of the water. The sound of the liquid spraying and his intense craving for a drink render him oblivious to everything else around him. Each moment feels like an eternity as the gritty feeling in his throat intensifies.

As the pale-yellow tone leisurely lifts, it becomes more translucent but still discolored. The stream is filled with an unwanted abundance of minerals, making it look questionable to drink.

As his thirst intensifies, it feels like his throat is engulfed in flames, increasing his irritability and impatience. He is on the verge of being unable to swallow and, gasping for air, chokes. His fingers grip the edge of the sink, and he taps them rhythmically to steady himself. With each hit of his fingertips, he invokes a countdown for the moment he can lap up the flow and quench his thirst. His excitement about the nearly clear water causes his eyes to grow larger with excitement.

He draws nearer to the spigot, sticking out his tongue in anticipation.

JUDGEMENT

Seven

WHAT'S IN THE BAG

As the image of the glistening water reflects off his dilating pupils, something is brewing behind him, taking advantage of his complacency.

Remaining unseen, a dark shadow slinks across the hallway's walls. Slowly creeping, it reaches the kitchen's ceiling and lingers overhead. Its black aura projects a mask, darkening the counter space. As it hovers over the mound of fetid garbage sacks, like a storm cloud, the cast shadow alters the bodily liquid that is pooling on the countertop. The goo's green hue intensifies and fizzles as tiny bubbles rise to its surface. Its vigorous nature resembles the boiling created by a feasting school of hungry piranhas on the attack. Silently working, the darkness turns the liquid's contents acidic as it devours the plastic, dissolving it layer by layer.

Each eroding package reveals its contents with a sudden *pop* reminiscent of opening a tube of refrigerator biscuits. Adonis's joke becomes a reality, as each bag contains the remains of a corpse. Women's bodies have been callously butchered to fit inside the confined spaces, rendering the parts almost unrecognizable as human.

The scene's brutality reveals the gruesome account of a perpetrator who completely disregards human life. The atrocity that has taken place is irredeemable. It is utterly horrifying.

Each bundle of mangled flesh and bone has been chopped and compressed into dense blocks using a trash compactor before being concealed inside the garbage bags. The only remaining recognizable part is the decomposing head. Whether by choice or because of the skull's thicker bone, it was kept mostly intact, with the brain and eyes still attached.

As the simmering goop engulfs the plastic, a putrid smell fills the air. Each piece of ebony flesh covering the bone is skillfully stitched together, with new patches replacing the old ones as they rotted away. The variety of textures and shades of ebony combine to mimic a child's art project.

Once the liquid has eaten away each of the outer wrappings, the bubbling ceases. The end of the fizzing indicates the assignment's completion, designed to release something more menacing.

Coming to life, the mismatched skull's jaw hinges open. As it silently yawns, its bones lock into place, and the eye impaled by the knife rolls in circles in an effort to free itself.

The room's energy causes the water's pressure to rise, forcing the last rust from the pipes. Adonis shoves his head under the faucet to cure his dehydration.

While he takes large gulps of water, the mounds of bone and meat rock back and forth; as the piles gain momentum, the fetid matter edges forward like a glut of slugs slithering toward the skull. They leave a slimy trail through the pool of bodily fluid.

Immediately, the eyes of the head dart to the right to stare at Adonis's back, and its teeth clack together, triggering movement inside the jaw. A tongue slowly uncoils, rolling from the back of its severed throat, and as the bulging organ extends fully into its mouth, the tip rises to the roof of the head's rotted palate, waiting for its time to escape.

Converging at the skull, every accumulation of flesh and bone heaves upon each other, constructing a mountain of decay on the counter.

As the corpse's head watches Adonis quenching his thirst, the woman's tongue wriggles, creating tiny clacks. Her subtle call causes the mountainous blob to stir like a tidal wave, rebuilding itself into a new shape. The ground fragments of human remains serve as a gelatinous conveyor, inching the head upward to take its rightful place at the top as if on a throne.

Feeling satisfied, Adonis pulls his head back from the stream of water to wipe his chin. "Oh, boy, was that good," he says, refreshed. Quickly pushing himself away from the sink, he straightens his posture and stretches his back as he yawns.

Behind him, the scene transforms into a horrifying spectacle as the entity takes shape. Beneath the skull, the once-nondescript blob is changing into the form of a woman.

Wrapping up his stretch, Adonis cracks his knuckles. He feels invincible and is ready to return the rancid contents to the freezer. "All right, time to get back to business." He glances at the running faucet, realizes he has forgotten something, and chuckles. "One thing at a time," he says, reaching for the sink's handle.

As he extends his hand toward the knob, the water abruptly stops. It catches him off-guard, reigniting his fear. Quickly trying to divert his attention, he prevents himself from overthinking by letting out an awkward laugh. "Huh. Well, I guess that's that," he says, giving a slight shrug. He clears his throat, but as he turns around, his optimism swiftly fades.

Nothing is as he left it.

The garbage bags have vanished, leaving behind trails of fetid sludge, and the shadows have become more pronounced, casting an eerie darkness over the room. Beyond the mayhem, something stirs in the silence.

As he stares at the scene, his mind runs wild. He knows that for the bundles to move, something must have been lurking behind him while he drank the water, and the thought of his obliviousness terrifies him.

The more he reflects on the situation, the more his mind becomes clouded with anxiety. He wants answers. He takes a deep breath to think, but his flustered state makes him frantic. "Who—who's there?" he asks.

Scanning the space for clues, he catches a slight movement, and his attention is drawn to the counter section beside the refrigerator.

Within the murkiest point of the shadow, the ill-assorted flesh tower, resembling the twisted form of a woman's physique, crouches, staring at him, eyes glowing in the darkness.

The putrid odor still lingers in the air, similar to before but more pungent. As he turns, sniffing to find the source, he glimpses a partially formed toe resting over the counter's edge. Adonis cannot look away, recoiling in disgust and horror as it squirms and writhes in the slimy goop that has escaped its packaging. He holds his breath, fighting the urge to retch as the sight and scent provoke him to vomit.

The aroma is unbearable, with nothing left to seal off the stench of decay. With every breath he takes, the astringent gas triggers his gag reflex and stings his eyes, causing his tear ducts to fill with water. He fans the air in front of his face, hoping to clear the smell from his nose. Soon, he will realize that the scent is the least of his worries.

"What the hell ..." he says, his hands shaking as he tries to make sense of the scene. He attempts to stay calm as he scans the figure from the bottom to the top, his eyes locking on her face.

Despite the rough quality of the patchwork, he finds himself entranced by its mesmerizing qualities and drawn to certain features that seem oddly familiar. As he stares at her, it provokes a surge of emotions within him. Not wanting to feel, he winces, trying to fight himself back into numbness. "Stop it, Adonis ... now's not the time," he says, shaking his head.

Though her eyes are cloudy and fixed narrowly past him, she watches his every move.

Not thinking that she notices, he seizes the moment and, trying to control his shaking, takes a tiny step back.

Slowly following his retreat, her right pupil spastically rolls in a figure-eight pattern, and as it lands, the opposite iris follows suit with a slight delay. As they finally settle to look in unison, the knife handle of the blade impaling the center of the recessed cornea points in his direction like the bent paw of a hunting dog.

He stares directly at the protruding object. The knife is surrounded by a dried, thick gunk, forming a crusty crater around the wound. Its resemblance to a bullseye draws him in. Goosebumps pile onto his arms, triggering each hair to stand on end. Trembling with fear, he is already one step ahead, his foot shifting further behind him to prepare for his escape.

She can sense every tremor coursing through him, and they make her innards tickle, and the corners of her lips curl. Her swollen tongue presses against the roof of her mouth as she prepares to speak. It forcefully pries her teeth open, allowing a raspy breath to exit her lungs. The burst of oxygen projects particles into the air, paving the way for her wail. "Don't you think I'm beautiful?" she asks; abruptly, her sadness turns to cynicism. The gory mess forming a neck twists to reveal her face, exhibiting a look of perplexity. "What's the matter?"

Her question makes him tense, leaving him at a loss for words. Fumbling, he stutters and takes an awkward step backward. "Nuh—I mean nothing. What's making you think something's wrong? There's nothing wrong. It's all good," he says, trying to remain inconspicuous; he avoids looking backward to check his footing, stumbling as he takes another step.

The woman's mouth twists into a grin. "Oh? Is that so? Then where are you going?" she asks. Her skin puckers as she speaks, highlighting the ill-stitched seams at the edges of her mouth.

Immediately knowing he has been caught, his nerves prompt sweat to form above his brow, and his heart races. He fixates on a drop of salty sweat dripping toward his eyelid and squinches his face to redirect it. "Nah, I'm not going anywhere, no way. I am digging... the view," he says. Taking a moment of pause, he slides his foot further behind him and takes another step backward.

With her pupils fixed, she watches him, and her grin deepens.

He studies her stare to see if she notices his slight movements to get away, and not detecting a response, he assumes his escape is going under the radar. Clearing his throat, he continues his slow retreat while using his words to create a distraction. "You see, I was ... was," he says, stammering; his chattering teeth provoke his mounting sweat to drip from his forehead and roll down his cheeks. He talks faster and nervously chuckles. "Um, oh boy, I mean, you're just so unique. I've never seen anyone quite like you before..."

Her ears wiggle, and her burgeoning tongue licks the front of every darkened tooth. His speech incites her fury, causing her jaw muscles to clench. The seething expression on her face makes her rotted eyelids flutter, and as the leathered skin of her left eye collides with the end of the lodged knife blade, it splices the upper portion down the center, creating two flaps.

Adonis's feet plant against the floorboards beneath him; he watches her left eye roll upward, back into her skull, sucking the blade further into the socket as if trying to swallow it whole. In a wave of confusion, his body shivers in horror.

The bone of her jaw produces a loud snap as it opens; something is squirming inside and trying to get out. He squints to focus on the movement. "What the..."

Starting as a trickle, a group of larvae tumbles from her gaping mouth to her tongue. As their numbers increase, they stack on top of each other, intensifying the force of their departure and resulting in a pile-up. Their abundance grows. Each new wave of insects pushes the ones in front, creating a cascade of falling worms from her bottom teeth, tumbling to the floor.

Adonis cannot take his eyes off the hoard of wriggling rice rapidly approaching his toes. The skittering sound of the maggots squirming and writhing across the wood is too much for him to bear. He shuffles backward, focusing on preventing them from touching his feet, until a loud *thud* redirects his attention to the counter.

The flesh and bone slurry making up the woman's silhouette has collapsed. As the once-compressed heap lies in a mound with the skull on top, its mouth spasms to rid itself of the remaining bugs.

With a vacant gaze, Adonis endeavors to wrap his head around the scene. His confusion is so overwhelming that he instinctively holds his breath, making it impossible to think clearly. Dizziness engulfs him, causing him to gasp for air, and, struggling to stay upright, he locks his knees.

The skull's mouth unhinges, moving side to side, each jarring twitch accompanied by a sharp crack. With each snap, his nerves are triggered, and he flinches. Although he knows the entity's state renders functional movement implausible, its unpredictability brings him terror.

The smell of death permeates the room's humidity. It is all he can focus on as it makes its way underneath his erratically flaring nostrils. Succumbing to his fear, he frantically looks behind him. Ready to run for it, his eyes dart around the room for a place to hide.

The door he had ripped from the closet remains on the floor a short distance from the broken doorframe, exactly where he had left it.

He focuses on the splintered ends and notices that each jagged shard silently sticks from the damaged wood. Every tip is highlighted by the daylight infiltrating the window. The eerie haze stresses the danger hidden behind them he had missed.

Their innocence has been stripped away by the door's removal, and they now appear like menacing spikes. The risk is alluring. Their sharpness calls to him, drawing him in.

He reflects on what it would be like to relinquish his total weight and fall on top of them, allowing them to take control of his fate. As his imagination stirs, his eyes gloss over. The thought of not being the driver of his destiny is highly enticing; it would relieve his guilt and provide an effortless escape from his tormented life.

The concept relaxes him, and the sadistic reality shuts him off from the world surrounding him, appearing before him as his only hope, and he becomes obsessed. He will do anything to chase a euphoric high.

Swiftly giving into his imagination, he allows his mind to wander further in his dark fantasy, visualizing every detail of the wooden spikes piercing his skin and the sensation of blood pouring to its surface. He pictures the crimson liquid soaking through his clothes and the warmth of being reborn, like a baptism washing away his pent-up sadness. The pain would allow him to cleanse his mind and purge his trauma once and for all.

That would be the end of it all. His mind would finally be left in silence.

Abruptly, a large wave crashes against the side of the houseboat. The sudden jolt breaks his thoughts and leaves him staring at the unhinged door.

Shaking his head, he looks around nervously. "What is wrong with you?" he says, realizing how genuinely dark his thoughts have become. "This isn't you," he whispers.

Everything in the room taunts him.

He shakes his head again, trying to rid his mind of the darkness. He had never considered harming himself before, and he struggles to differentiate his organic thoughts from the tricks brought on by the house's control. "This isn't a game, you sick fuck!" he shouts with all his might for his captor to hear, tears welling up in his eyes. Trapped and unable to think clearly, he releases a guttural scream of frustration.

Unexpectedly, he catches sight of movement from the corner of his eye, drawing his attention toward the disassembled woman's body. He realizes he may not have time to get to the bedroom entrance to find a hiding spot, and standing in the middle of the kitchen's open space elicits a feeling of panic. He has nowhere to hide if she reassembles.

In a moment of quick decision-making, he determines he has only one option to ensure that she will not pose a threat in the future, and that is to eliminate the possibility of her return. He needs to take care of her himself.

Simultaneously, the flesh beneath the skull boils and bubbles, sending gas clouds floating upward, traveling through the stagnant air. The putrid stench assaults his nostrils, causing his stomach to turn, and he reflexively pinches his nose. As he looks toward the awaiting head, he is confronted by the one-eyed glare of the decomposing skull. Their gaze locks, and the bubbles seem to lose their speed.

His eyes dart nervously toward the floor where the maggots writhe and squirm. Their slimy bodies crawl on top of one another. It makes him cringe in disgust. "You can do it," he says, forcing a deep breath of tainted air to calm his nerves; he continues his pep talk. "Just gotta move fast and keep looking ahead."

The insects migrate, dispersing across a larger radius.

He briefly closes his eyes and takes another breath. As they reopen, they are greeted with the tongue of the corpse wiggling and spewing chants, summoning the pulverized body parts to regroup.

Without hesitation, he springs into action, his body darting forward. "Oh—hell, no, you don't," he says. Maggots are crushed under his feet as he sprints across the room, not bothering to watch where he steps—their bodies release chaotic popping sounds with each tramp of his loafers. The crunching noise disgusts him, making him want to vomit.

Clenching his jaw, he keeps his eye on his target and, extending his arm, grabs a handful of her matted curls. With a single swift motion, he plucks the skull from the pile and holds it as far as possible away from his body.

The head swings from side to side, her teeth gnashing at the air. He winces, startled by the clashing of her molars. Worried he will get bitten, he becomes apprehensive and unconsciously loosens his grip. "Oh, no, nope. Oh, hell no!" he says. His eyes widen as he realizes what he is doing, and he swiftly tightens his hold to avoid dropping it.

A sinister look spreads across her face as her mouth twists into a demonic grin. "What a handsome boy," she says.

In a split second, he darts to the freezer, kicking bugs off his feet with each stride. As he opens the door, he gives her one last look and, repulsed, tosses the head inside. An ominous growl forms within the appliance, and the head slowly swivels itself around on the shelf.

Not taking any chances, he slams the door shut. The door's movement pushes the air, sending a gust of warmth in his direction. "Shit," he says, thinking the power is going out again; he pounds the front of the deep freeze. "C'mon. Don't fail me now. It's already rank enough in here." He says.

The surrounding temperature continues to climb as the vents blow, searing hot air.

A whoosh of heat brushes the back of his neck, and noticing his clothing is becoming damp with perspiration, he realizes the problem is more extensive than he had thought.

The hot gusts from the heater vents billow out, forming a thick humidity that lingers around him.

Unable to ignore it, he looks toward the square-shaped exhausts. "Come on, cut me some slack," he says, noticing a heat rash on his skin. He glances back toward the refrigerator and catches his reflection staring back at him through the condensation on its once-glossy surface. His blurred state makes it appear as if he is melting.

The room is so hot that it mimics an oven set on preheat. Removing his fedora, he wipes the sweat from his forehead. "Think, think, think," he says, wincing from the heat.

As another blast of air exits the vent, it carries the sound of clacking metal. His reddening eyes drift to look. "Well, that can't be good," he says, placing his hat snugly on his head.

The room's temperature continues to climb, bringing the pulverized remains on the counter to a roasting simmer. He sniffs upon detecting a faint aroma of the putrid meat cooking. Then he hears a low sizzle humming in his ear. The sludge beneath the mounds of flesh froths vigorously as it fries at full speed on the countertop, reaching the temperature of frying oil in a cast iron skillet.

His overloaded senses fuel his anger, and he snaps. He channels his frustration, pounding his fist against the deep freeze. The exerted energy causes the veins to bulge in his neck as he shouts at the top of his lungs, "You happy, man? Have you seen what happens when a dead body bakes in the sun? Do you have any clue what that smells like? Do you? Let me tell you. It's worse than someone taking a shit on your clothes and forcing you to wear them in the scorching Louisiana summer."

The foul liquid's boiling creates a whistle as the gas exits between the fragments of tendon and bone.

He sarcastically laughs to drown out the annoyance and shakes his head. Determined to get his point across, he continues, "Hold up ... I'm not done... "

With each second that passes, the high-pitched whine becomes more aggressive.

Pushed to the brink, he resolutely avoids wiping away the sweat on his face so as not to break his momentum, wholly absorbed in his mission to convey his beliefs to his captor. The pace of his speech escalates. "You get that this space isn't that big, right? Huh? It's only a matter of time before this God-awful smell travels to wherever you're hiding. So, that means we'll suffer together—not just me, we." His voice cracks as his lungs take in more of the dank air. "Like it or not, we will both be stuck in the same shit dump-smelling living space."

The boiling liquid on the countertop hisses and sputters, sending blackened bits of flesh flying.

Tightly shutting his eyes, he sighs; perspiration drenches his shirt. The lack of corroboration frustrates him, and grunting, he takes a moment to stew in his anger and sweat. He clenches his fists and lowers his voice to a whisper. "You sick motherfucker!" He says.

The more time that elapses, the worse the issue becomes; the heat escalates, and the aroma intensifies. He is frantic to find relief; all he can think about is eliminating the putrid smell, and knowing he must devise a plan to dampen the stench, he reluctantly pivots to face the countertop.

The sight of the meat has shifted. The boiling goop has seared the flesh, partially cooking it, removing some of its transparency.

He quickly looks at the freezer. "Yeah, that'll work," he says, shrugging. Convinced of his foolproof idea, he confidently declares, "It has a seal ... I just have put everything back inside where I found it, and it will take care of itself."

Before he can finish his thought, he gives the freezer's handle a heavy tug.

It does not budge.

Unbeknownst to him, opening and closing it earlier has resulted in a vacuum.

He refuses to acknowledge that his plan may have already failed. Forcing a smile, the muscles in his cheeks quiver. "Oh, hell no, you don't. Not today. We're not doing this today," he says, glaring at the resistant handle. He desperately tugs at the door with even greater force, but it remains uncooperative.

His face reddens with effort, and his body responds by sweating more profusely. "Come on..." he says, pleading. Refusing to admit defeat, each erratic movement triggers his legs' sweaty skin to stick to the material of his wool pants, causing him to feel even more trapped. As stress hives afflict his belly, the sensory overload makes him squirm, and, wanting it to end, he tugs even harder, causing his arms to quiver uncontrollably.

The door refuses to budge, no matter how much muscle he puts into it. Irritable and exhausted, he finally lets go, his clammy palms stinging as they mix with sweat and hot air. Glancing at the tender skin, he notices it has peeled and blistered. The forceful friction against the handle has rubbed them raw. As he fixates on the damage, the pain becomes unbearable, and he screams in agony, spewing spit and kicking the freezer, resulting in a stubbed toe. "I can't catch a break," he says, hopping on one foot.

A rattle sounds from the vent above, followed by a gust of air that carries a burst of faint laughter. It haunts him as it echoes through the room. He cringes at the prickly, mocking essence of the noise as it contributes to the chaos and exacerbates his deteriorating mental state. Battling his emotions, he clenches his jaw to suppress his tears. "You think this is funny?" he asks, sniffing and looking at the ground.

The wooden floorboards are littered with motionless maggots. As the heat makes him light-headed, he leans forward, giving him a closer look at the tiny insects. He watches the drops of sweat drip from his forehead, soaking their lifeless bodies.

Their lack of transparency shows that the heat has cooked them alive.

Although the thought of not having them as an obstacle brings him happiness, his joy is short-lived. As the temperature continues to climb, the addition of a throbbing headache causes his sense of defeat to return. "Take that," he says, punting the hardened carcasses across the floor as anger rushes through him. Their tiny bodies create little tapping sounds as they hit against the wood cabinetry.

He gradually slips into a state of delirium, and as the dizziness overtakes him, he staggers to keep his balance as everything becomes hazy. As his hunger pains worsen, a growl rolls through the pit of his stomach. He chuckles to hide the discomfort caused by the ache. "Ah, screw it, I'll just deal with the stink a little longer," he says; switching gears, he ravenously stumbles toward the cabinets and reaches for the first door. "If I'm gonna die, the least the guy can do is feed me first."

Upon opening the cabinet, he discovers an empty shelf adorned with discolored yellow flower-patterned paper and sticky residue rings left by long-gone cans. His stomach rumbles louder, irritating him, and he rushes to the next door in line without bothering to close the door. He frantically pulls it open, only to find a single shelf that looks identical to the last.

When he is about to move on, he spots a shadow, causing him to freeze in place. Without hesitation, he reaches to the back of the shelf, and the feeling of something metal makes his eyes dilate.

The object has absorbed the excessive temperatures, rendering it searing to the touch. Even though it scorches his skin, his stomach pains take over, and, ignoring his burning fingertips, he drags out the item to get a better look. It is a large, slightly rusted, cylindrical tin container with a label that has been worn with time. Quickly, he adjusts his fingers to the tiny bits of the remaining paper sticker, protecting them from the heat as he turns the can for a better look.

The label's light brown coloring and torn brand name are both recognizable. Even though it is hard to read, excitement fills his eyes; he knows precisely what it is. "Hot cocoa, come to Papa," he says. "This stuff never goes bad."

Drool puddles at the corners of his lips as his fingers caress the lid, ready to open it.

Then he notices something odd: the cap is slightly lifted from the rim. Considering his previous experiences, he contemplates tampering.

Skepticism drives his conflicted thoughts as he ponders the risk of someone altering the can's contents versus the risk of going hungry. But, with no other options and hunger driving his decisions, he overlooks the idiosyncrasy and races toward the sink with it in his hand. Peeling the lid from the container, he chucks it over his shoulder and, imagining the taste of chocolate reaches for the sink handle.

A high-pressure stream of water shoots from the nozzle.

Sticking his head over the sink, he scoops a heap of dark powder from the container. Mindlessly shoving the dry mixture into his mouth, he uses his hand to redirect the gushing liquid behind his teeth, and his tongue sloshes to mix it. He swiftly swallows. Instead of calming his stomach, the taste startles him; it does not match what he remembers.

Rather than the sweet taste of chocolaty sugar, it is laced with the bitterness of gritty ash. The unappetizing texture is like a crushed, stale, burned marshmallow.

Immediately, he feels sick. Puffing his cheeks, he spits the remnants left on his palate into the sink, but the taste lingers; bits are stuck between his teeth. He tilts his head and watches the blackened gunk drift down the gurgling drain. Consumed by horror and confusion, he stares into the container, his vision unsteady. "What the..." His words are barely comprehensible.

Though the tin is recognizable, the contents are not. Instead of a rich cocoa brown color, the powder is a deep shade of black and gray with small, unidentified chunks mixed in. Unsure of what he has ingested, he panics and, opening his mouth, mumbles, "What ... what did you do to me?" Everything looks foggy as he feels the room spin, and, fighting his fading vision, he shouts, "Answer me!"

A deep laugh floods the room, the bass tone quaking the woodwork. It seeps into his ears, yanking at his psyche like a dog on a leash and thrusting him into a state of hyperventilation.

The voice grows louder, taking on a tone of something far more sinister. Each sound it produces rattles his nerves, spinning him deeper into a fragile state of mind. He cannot take it any longer. An insidious feeling gnaws at his consciousness like a parasite making its home inside his skull. Trying to fight the threat, he screams at the top of his lungs. "Goddammit, I said, answer me!"

Abruptly, a nearby floorboard loudly creaks. He jumps, and the idea of something lurking behind him sends a chill down his spine. Overcome with fear, he relies solely on his adrenaline as he spins around to examine his surroundings, but when his foot lands on the crunchy maggots, he slips and loses his grip on the tin can.

As momentum takes hold of the metal, guiding its direction, the can soars into the air, erupting powder and creating a polluted cloud that slowly drifts to the ground.

Adonis's body hits the floor, and the impact knocks the wind out of his lungs. Gasping for air, he inhales a wave of ash. As he struggles to breathe, his attention darts to his surroundings in search of the can.

Still descending, the heavy tin gains momentum from above and collides with his skull.

With the sudden blow, the last of his vision leaves, and his ears ring. As his consciousness drifts away, darkness floods his sight.

Eight

AMNESIA

Yet again, he is alone, surrounded by nothing but silence.

Time no longer exists during his blackout, and the days morph into one.

As Adonis's eyelids lightly flutter open, they are met with indescribable darkness. Even though his body is where it had dropped, facing the ceiling, and sprawled across the kitchen floor, he is unsure of where he is since he cannot make out anything around him. It is so dark that he is uncertain if his eyes are open or closed, and the unknown fuels his worst fears.

The room is still; there are no voices or signs of movement.

As he slowly focuses on his breaths, he regains bits of consciousness, picking up where everything left off with the addition of a throbbing headache.

The nuisance of running water leisurely trickling from the kitchen sink creates an irritating white noise. It consumes his attention. Each drop in the basin feeds his headache and makes him wince. He is unsure of what has occurred; all he can recall are jumbled bits and pieces contradicting one another.

Unlike the unbearable heat he remembered, the room's temperature is now freezing cold. Although he cannot see what is in front of his nose, he can feel each breath producing an icy residue that burns his nostrils when he inhales. He tries not to get too hung up on the differences as he struggles to shift his weight to his elbows and prop himself up.

From his slightly elevated position, he notices a peculiar sparkle of light. The wind has shifted the clouds, temporarily unveiling the radiant moon glow. It offers a pillar of hope amid the darkness, drawing him in like a moth to a flame as it shimmers in the left corner of his peripheral vision.

As each ray shines through the living room window, slivers of light scatter across the floor. A single speckle lands on his loafer, illuminating the tip of the toe.

Noticing a scuff-like mark on the snakeskin pattern, he licks his thumb, and while bending forward to wipe it, he stops himself; something about it looks off. Leery of the accuracy of his hazy vision, he quickly blinks to sharpen his sight.

There is an unusual depth to the color. Although it appears black from a distance, bits of the warm lighting from the moon unveil the actual hue of the dark stain.

He shimmies his body closer to get a better view, and then, turning his shoe back and forth under the light, he studies the details.

Upon closer examination, the black reveals a tinge of deep burgundy, darkest at the center of the smear and gradually fading toward the edges, creating a subtle crimson transparency.

Though he may not initially acknowledge that he knows what it is, his subconscious is fully aware of the reality.

Seeking more proof, he gradually rotates his heel. As his toe moves further into the light's path, his skin flushes, and his body stiffens.

A strand of curly hair catches the light as it sticks out from the thick substance at the center of the stain.

Even as all his what-ifs are ripped from his psyche, the thought of it being gore still startles him, and paranoia sets in regarding what else may be hidden as the clouds shift again, leaving him surrounded by darkness.

He leans away from his shoe, and the shift prompts a muffled rattle in his pocket. The noise triggers his memory of the spilled drawer. Swiftly, he rummages inside his coat and pulls out the box of matches. "I knew you'd come in handy," he says, holding it between his trembling fingers as he fumbles to open it.

Unable to keep it still, each small stick collides, creating a subtle clatter. "Focus," he says, trying to stop his shaking while still obsessing over the stain on his shoe. Finally, making a small opening, he fishes inside the box, retrieving a single match. He glides his fingertips across the exterior and finds the worn friction strip on the side. Not wasting a moment, he strikes the match to light it.

A tiny flame grows to a dancing flicker at the end of the stick. As he holds the minuscule torch near his chilled skin, it projects a warmth that feels like needles jabbing into his flesh. His attention shifts to the glow of the match, exposing something on the tips of his fingers.

The scarlet substance is not just isolated to his shoe; it also paints the beds of his fingernails. Just as he thinks it can't get any worse, his despair deepens as he realizes something is trapped in a tiny crack on his thumbnail - another delicate strand of hair.

Based on its length, he knows it does not belong to him. "What, what did you do?" he asks, staring in disbelief at the discovery. "Dear God, what did I do? "

His heart pounding, he fixates on the crimson stains, unable to look away from the alarming state of his hands. Their disturbing condition creates a sense of detachment as if he is watching himself from a distance. As he moves the tiny flame closer, his eyes widen in fear.

The first match dies, and he strikes another. The flame continues devouring the stick, and little by little, its bright essence reveals more of the grotesque display.

In denial, he cannot look away, and almost like he's having an out-of-body experience, the longer he stares, the more he disconnects. Each tiny detail does not seem like his own; it registers in his mind as a stranger. Picking out flaws, he finds the fingers are more weathered with age and the skin thicker, callused like leather. Each feature holds his attention as he hyper-focuses, unable to look away.

The second match dies, and he strikes another.

The flame works faster, eating away at the wood as if counting down the seconds to his mental breakdown. He nervously rotates it and then pinches the bottom of the stick with more pressure. "This must be another one of his tricks," he laughs. "Yeah ... yup, that's it."

Fueled by the small bits of tinder, the tiny flame grows taller. Although the heat should warn him it is getting dangerously close to his skin, his obsession with its dancing movement overtakes him, and he allows the darkness to infect his mind. Every puff of black smoke that leaves from the hypnotizing orange flicker produces a soft crackle; the sound is orgasmic, like a sea of whispers in his ears.

He is envious of its effortless movements because, unlike him, it is free. Wanting to mimic it, he gives in to the intoxicating pull, and as he falls into a dreamy trance, a peculiar fascination grips him: he imagines the sensation of fire caressing his skin.

The third match dies, and he strikes another.

To see his skin melt away and his fiery flesh turn to dust may satisfy his longing for accomplishment. The belief of achieving anything, even if it means ending his life, could fill the void of his enduring lack of purpose, regardless of its macabre nature.

Every wiggling movement of the fire grows in beauty. Its mesmerizing luster in the darkness ushers his pupils to expand, revealing a glimpse into the depths of his soul.

Consumed by his thoughts, he remains oblivious to the flame grazing his skin.

Suddenly, the pain from its burn sends a signal of panic through his nervous system that snaps him from his fantasy. He swiftly moves his fingers to the farthest end of the stick.

Realizing the fire is almost out and fearing the dark, he becomes frantic, and his hand fumbles to retrieve another match from the box.

He lights the new flame with the old, then releases the charred stick of the fourth match and twists it into the floor. It quickly extinguishes, and all that is left is a tiny ember.

Upon its disappearance, a void settles within him, intensifying his awareness of being alone. "Pull yourself together, man," he says, closing his eyes and attempting to focus on the sound of the running water, only to realize it has stopped.

An unsettling silence surrounds him.

The peace is short-lived, destroyed by a high-pitched squeak resonating behind him. It brings him back to the moment of rummaging through the cupboards. Even though he refuses to look, he recognizes it; it is coming from the hinges of one of the cabinet doors in the kitchen.

With each clench of his jaw, he feels a wave of numbness wash over him. The pressure in his head is getting worse because of the can's impact, desensitizing him to the situation and making his mind even more confused.

The hairs on his arms stand slowly as random bits of knowledge from the past flash through his mind. "Remember, none of this is real," he says with apprehension. "It's all a game."

The groan of the hinges grows louder as the door to the cabinet continues to open. Then, with a significant thrust, it crashes into the wood, causing him to recoil. He quakes as he opens the match container and grabs another from the box. "What's the worst it can be?" he asks.

The fifth match dies, and he strikes another.

With the tiny torch gripped between his fingers, he leads the way with it, using it to light the way as he scoots to face the sound's direction. Its glow illuminates a small radius. He extends his arm further to better understand what is before him.

The hinges of the cupboard release a squeal. Quickly, his gaze darts toward the noise, and, expecting to be met with a swinging cabinet door, he is startled by the movement of something different rustling in the dark. His complexion turns pale, and tremors roll through his body; the quaking of his hand nearly extinguishes the flame. He silently observes it, taking a moment to steady himself.

Irrespective of the angle, the cupboard door obstructs his sight of what appears to be a person of medium stature hunching over and digging deep into the back of the cabinet.

Frustrated by the limited view, he becomes increasingly impatient in his quest for answers. As the match dwindles between his fingers, he resists the urge to give up his observation and lights match number seven.

Edging closer, he now has a clearer view of the person's traits that indicate their masculine identity.

He nervously clears his throat and, unsure if he should speak, keeps his volume in a whisper. "Hello?" he asks. His words are barely audible.

As his eyes anxiously dart around the room, he notices a glistening on the ground. The match's flickering flame is reflecting off something on the floor.

As the subtle glow illuminates the outer edge of the residue, it reveals footprints made of swamp water and mud.

Carefully adjusting the light source, he stays motionless as his eyes scan the tracks, beginning with the one closest to him. When he reaches the end, the prints traversing the kitchen floor leave no mystery to whom they belong—they lead directly to the man. His fishing waders are drenched, with the water dripping from the cuffs and forming a murky pool around his feet.

As his eyes stumble back to the stranger's dirty waders, the man's imposing stature renders him speechless; unease settles within him. He cannot help but wonder if the individual in front of him is responsible for his captivity and torment.

The seventh match dies, and he lights another.

With bated breath, he intently observes the man as he leans forward on the tips of his toes and delves deeper into the cabinet, the rubber soles of his boots squeaking on the floorboards.

Adonis's jaw clenches, and a knot forms in his stomach. Watching the man fills him with a sense of foreboding as if he has stumbled upon something he was never meant to see; everything in his head tells him to run. Regardless, he ignores his intuition.

In his gut, he knows the man is his captor, and he should be excited about the confrontation coming to fruition. But finally, having him in his grasp, the idea of facing him terrifies him, and he cannot muster the courage to speak. The man's presence provokes flashbacks of all he has endured and what he has seen; it makes him feel weak and sends shivers down his spine.

The flame eating away at the match silently creeps down the stick. An unexpected wave of emotion overcomes him, and rather than just rage, it brings sadness. The conflicting emotions amplify his inner turmoil, and the overwhelming sensation immobilizes him, pushing his nervous system to the verge of collapse. Even though he senses the heat reaching his fingertips, his limbs will not cooperate to address it.

Helplessly, he watches the scene unfold, his eyes widening as the boots exhibit another sign of movement.

The eighth match dies, and he lights another.

Swaying forward, the man inches further onto his toes, prompting more of his upper torso to disappear into the cabinet. His search becomes more frantic, and as he pats the empty areas, his palms create a *thud, thud, thud* that resonates through the kitchen. Every brutal slap makes Adonis wince; it sounds like a drum beginning a ritual.

Not finding what he is looking for, the man becomes frustrated and loudly grunts. The raspy howl creates an echo that rounds the emptiness of the wooden cupboard and, finding its way out, projects into the open room. Growing increasingly agitated over his fruitless search, the man clambers onto his knees atop the countertop, stretching upward to gain better access to the cabinet.

Hearing the noise of the man's kneecaps sliding on the sludge-covered surface triggers Adonis's recollection of earlier.

The tempo of the rhythmic smacks becomes quicker.

As he focuses on the flashback, Adonis remembers pillaging the cabinets for food. The closer he gets to recollecting the last moments of his discovery, the more he notices a chalky ash taste lingering on his tastebuds. "Hot ... the hot chocolate..." he says, stammering. The horrible thought of the black sludge collecting on his tongue and wedging between his teeth turns his stomach.

Knowing all the other cabinets are bare, he realizes what the man wants: he is looking for the tin.

Upon the ninth match's demise, Adonis retrieves two from the box, igniting one and clutching the other.

Immediately, the last instant of his fall floods his mind when the cocoa tin slipped from his fingers, and the stale powdery mix scattered through the air. His heart races as he wonders how long it will be before his captor realizes what he has done.

The fire burns faster down this matchstick than the others, almost touching his fingernail.

His paranoia worsens, and a sinking feeling plagues his gut. Afraid of the stranger's wrath, he knows he must find the can. Without sudden movements, his pupils shift to the furthest point his eyes will allow. Quickly scanning the darkness, he looks for where it could have landed.

Consumed by his search, he remains oblivious as a small fire quietly eats away at his fingernail and callused finger-tips. It blisters his skin, triggering a sharp pain that removes his defenses. In agony, he screams at the top of his lungs, releasing both matches from his hands.

The matches tumble to the ground. The ignited one lands on a swampy footprint, and the unlit one falls just out of the water's reach.

Frantically wanting relief, Adonis holds the tip of his burned thumb in his fist to cool the burn. As it ceases, he hears the fizzling of the flame and realizes what he has done.

The room falls pitch black. Left in complete darkness, he shivers with fear. "Shit, shit, shit, shit," he says, frantic; he scrambles to retrieve another match from his pocket.

But all that remains is an empty container.

The silent shake of the shallow box causes a tremble to roll over his body. "Stupid, why did you do that? What were you thinking?" he asks himself. His frustration compounds as he realizes that his last match was lost while he tended to his injury. He strains to survey the floor for it, but he can't see anything. Everything is too dark.

The cabinet door that was left open abruptly shuts, producing a shattering crash. Adonis jumps.

He knows he has little time and anxiously pats the floor around his body. "Come on ... you couldn't have gone far," he says. His movement is accompanied by a palpable wave of terror, causing him to quicken his pace.

The man waits near the cabinet; he has not moved. He is using the darkness to his advantage. Remaining stagnant, a trickle of water makes its way from his fishing boot onto the wooden floor, creating an eerie drip.

Even though he knows deep down his captor has not left, Adonis wishfully thinks the stillness means he can forget about him, but that is not the case. The motionlessness offers no safety as the drips resonate like a ticking clock, counting down the seconds of his life.

Darkness only adds to the uncertainty as he scrambles faster, searching for anything to provide light.

The room grows frigid as the man's wading boots drip slowly, methodically—*drip ... drip...drip.*

Anticipating hearing footsteps, Adonis's heart races and his eyes bulge in fear. Already pushed to his limits, he does not know how much more he can take. "Please," he says, begging for a matchstick to appear; his desperation causes his fingers to shake uncontrollably as he is met with his worst fear.

Something is approaching. His captor is on the move.

Struggling to catch his breath, Adonis can barely hold himself together, and upon hearing a second footfall, he lets out a whimper of panic. On the verge of surrender, his palm encounters the stray rigid matchstick, and he forces his trembling fingers to seize it. Not having time to retrieve the box, he squeezes his numb grip tighter and begins striking it against the toe of his shoe.

As the situation intensifies, becoming more dire, a collection of whispering voices arises out of thin air. "You're out of time. You better run," they say, taunting him. Every word they utter hisses and growls, reminiscent of a python being devoured alive. The voices carry an indescribable darkness as if they are summoning something, while their tones alternate between shrieks and whispers.

Adonis wildly strikes the match with more conviction, and the shoe's friction finally triggers it to light. He lifts it to eye level, chuckling in disbelief. Each movement of the tiny flame fills him with hope.

A single high-pitched voice brings a tone of demonic evil from front and center. It stands out from the rest. There is no gender in the voice; it purely exists, creating chaos in the air.

A droplet of saliva lands on Adonis's earlobe, triggering angst to boil in his gut. His body trembles with such intensity that the match nearly slips from his hand. He battles against his reluctance to reply, clenching his jaw tightly before finally mustering the courage to speak. "You can't control me!" He yells.

Jumping to his feet, he defiantly raises the flickering light to eye level.

His momentary courage is swiftly extinguished, instantly giving way to terror as he stares with his jaw hanging open at his captor. The only thing keeping their noses from touching is the match's flame.

The scent of death permeates his breath, reminiscent of a body left to rot in the bayou on a hot summer's day. Silence washes over the room, stopping the whispers, leaving only the sound of the man's disjointed wheezing.

As Adonis feels the heat of his breath and his gaze intensifies, he is consumed by helplessness. He oddly finds familiarity in the shape of the man's pupils; they exude a strange sense of stability, numbing his nerves. Even though he still senses looming danger, something inside the dark irises takes the edge off his worry.

Slowly, the man's lips part, suggesting an intention to speak. Paired with his mouth's movement, the shape of his eyes shifts.

The two men's proximity limits Adonis's view of the man's lower face. Catching the far corners of his lips widening, he wants to hear what his captor has to say. As he prepares to hinge his mouth shut, he panics; his jaw muscles are locked, almost as if the bones have been fused.

The outer edges of the man's eyes wrinkle.

Adonis fights to control the muscles of his face as his tongue frenetically wiggles in his open mouth. The sensation of air blowing past his teeth and tickling his larynx makes him realize he is dangerously vulnerable; he is trapped inside a body he cannot control. "Help," he says, but none of his words are audible. His call is dampened by spit pooling in his throat.

As his captor watches him struggle, his obsidian black irises constrict. Terrified of the unknown, Adonis stares at the man's shifting eyes as an overwhelming fear consumes him. He fixates on the idea of his freedom being taken from him. Powerless to move, he struggles to resist, but his body remains frozen in place.

The stranger's tongue elongates, rolling from his mouth and plunging forward, snatching the match from his captive's fingertips like a lizard and swallowing it whole.

Abruptly, everything goes dark.

As the light is taken away, Adonis's body goes limp, falling to his knees like a marionette dropped by its puppeteer; it makes it impossible for him to fight back. He refuses to allow himself to blink, filling his ducts with liquid as he labors to determine the man's distance. Tears overflow his lids, forging paths down his cheeks. They tumble in his pried-open mouth, pooling in his look of misery. Nervously, he strains to detect the man's breathing amid his muffled sobs.

The stranger's raspy inhalations and wheezing dissipate, revealing a voice identical to his own. "Hello, Adonis," he says. "I've been waiting for this moment for a very long time."

Plagued with confusion, he spirals into panic, his eyes fluttering and his tongue wriggling erratically as he tries to speak. Still fighting to keep his eyes open, he feels a cold sensation sweeping the top of his lids, ushering them to close.

The man's deep laughter resonates from the depths of his throat, humming as it passes through one ear and out the other. At the conclusion of his hilarity, he takes a lengthy inhale, each slurp of chilled air consuming more of Adonis's energy.

Clutching Adonis's head into his hands, he forcefully pulls him closer, and with his lips to his ear, he whispers, "You may think I'm a stranger." Lightly tapping his chest, he continues, "But we are alike in more ways than you know. That's where I live, inside of you."

The tone of the stranger's voice is like his own, and unable to see the man's lips moving, the similarity messes with Adonis's mind. He cannot determine if it is a thought coming from his head or the person in front of him. Regardless, the familiarity has a calming effect that sends comfort sweeping over him, covering him like a heated blanket and removing the goosebumps from his chilled body and limbs.

As he succumbs, the man's words become more urgent. "Our mistakes are all meant to test us! What is your price tag? Do you place an ounce of value on your life? That is the only thing that sets us apart, you and me. It is our determination not to let the trivial things determine our worth. Your downfall is driven solely by weakness."

As the voice trails off, Adonis's body flinches and spasms uncontrollably, sending him into withdrawal and shock. With each convulsion, he slumps further forward. A light foam bubbles up from his throat, and he coughs violently, spewing froth.

A loud whisper repeats from the darkness surrounding him. "Welcome to hell...to hell...to hell," it says.

He panics as the man grabs his ankles, and the friction of his pants against his tender skin reignites the pain in his wounds. His hands wrap tighter around his bony legs, and he gives them a hard yank. The swift motion causes Adonis to crash backward, his head making a sickening crack as it hits the floor.

With another heave, the man effortlessly drags his body behind him like a rag doll. As he tries to make sense of the situation, the sound of heavy footsteps reverberates through the floor, accompanied by a strange tune drifting through the air. The stranger's whistle gets louder with each tug, its eerie allure all too recognizable.

Piecing things together, Adonis realizes it is the same song the creature from the swamp had been singing, and, stricken with terror, his heart pounds in his chest. He recognizes it as a threatening warning, and he must get away.

Pushing through the pain, he regains movement in his arms. His hands flail wildly as if trying to grasp the darkness for stability. As he is forcefully dragged through the kitchen, he desperately paws for the cabinets surrounding him. In an attempt to create resistance and slow himself down, he grabs hold of a knob. As he tightens his grip, a loud *thud* against the side of the house startles him, causing him to let loose of his hold. Now, with no way to control his trajectory, his chin clips the edge of the base of the cabinet, snapping his jaw shut.

One by one, the *thump* repeats as additional birds hit the houseboat. As they crash into the wood, their beaks create chip marks in the siding, and their corpses tumble to the wooden deck, where their lungs convulse.

The excruciating pain in his jaw has left Adonis on edge, causing him to react defensively to the commotion; it sounds like war surrounds him in the pitch-black room. Disoriented and unsure of what direction the noise is coming from, his hands frantically rush to protect his head. As he attempts to shield himself from unseen forces, his captor drags his body out of the kitchen and into the living room.

Specks of warm light on the walls grab his attention, and he tilts his head to catch sight of one of the couches' legs. The thought of being in the space he is most familiar with brings a sense of security; he knows the layout. He finally feels he could have an advantage, but his confidence quickly fades as he looks toward the window.

The moon sheds light on a gruesome mess, illuminating the bright red smears of fresh blood, feathers, and bits of broken beaks left behind on the glass.

Frozen in shock, he can almost taste the sour essence of iron and smell their blood. Frantically, he looks away to clear the image from his mind, and his bruised jaw sends jolts of pain through his neck. Despite his efforts to detach himself from the scene, the image continues to evoke intense emotions within him, causing him to whimper and his mind to be filled with terrifying visuals of the tiny faces in their last moments. The thought of their fear upon impact makes him cringe.

He cannot help wondering if he will be next.

THE DEVIL

Nine

UNHINGED

The idea that his life might end causes his heart to pound faster. Believing he has nothing to lose, he lifts his head off the floor in his delirium to get a better look at the man dragging him.

His jailer pauses between steps. He shifts his weight, and the wet shell of his waders creates a rubbery squeak. A pair of wide brown suspenders keeps his baggy fishing trousers from falling off his body. It appears that the attire does not belong to him—or, more cynically, he purposely has chosen two sizes too large to disguise himself.

Adonis's neck becomes kinked as he strains to look, exacerbating his jaw pain and triggering nausea. Even though, from the back, the man's ill-fitting clothes skew his stature, he knows what is underneath; he has seen the sizes in his closet, and, surveying his height, he realizes they are relatively similar in proportion.

With another heave, his captor drags him a little further, the man's knuckles turning pale from the force of his grip.

His torturous grasp triggers pain from a prior injury Adonis had forgotten about. Struggling to hide his reaction, he locks his eyes on the stranger's hands, desperate to redirect his focus from the pain. As the moonlight penetrates the window, it lands on the man's knuckles, exposing a dark red hue.

He has constructed an impression of the man's appearance using the old photo he discovered in the kitchen drawer. As he looks at him in the dim lighting, he finds the youthful nature of his hands surprising; he had expected them to look more aged.

Amid his spiraling thoughts, the toe of his shoe catches his eye. The stain has not moved and has become darker, developing a more intense burgundy shade as oxidation has taken place.

Suddenly, the elevated position of his feet causes a tingling sensation to run down his legs, fueling his anxiety. He tentatively moves his hands in front of his face to see if the blood he discovered earlier is still there. Mixed with a few patches of charred skin, the gore remains, and the coiled lock is still wedged in his thumbnail.

The image reignites his unease. Like before, his thoughts about them have not changed; aside from the obvious, something feels off. It is almost as if he is staring at the hands of a stranger.

Flipping them over, he fights to steady his trembling. As he lifts his hands further in the air to get a better glimpse under the moonlight, gravity takes hold of his jacket sleeves, and they fall to his forearms.

There are matching injuries on each of his wrists.

His gaze locks on the horrifying details, unable to accept what he sees. It is as though he is having an out-of-body experience. The entire circumference of each wrist is crudely sutured. Each thick stitch holds the skin of his palm to the base of his arm, and the flesh surrounding the deep gashes is profoundly swollen and bruised. The wounds appear hacked, unevenly spaced, and infected.

The man whistles more sharply, growing louder. He appears to be quite chipper.

Adonis remains fixated on his wounds, causing him to be propelled into a state of shock, with his ashen face displaying the wave of horror sweeping over him. He frantically scans his memory for when the horrid act could have occurred but comes up with nothing but gaps. As the full extent of the agony sets in, his body uncontrollably shakes. His eyes glance back at his captor's hands tightening on him as he jerks his ankles. With more force than before, the aggressive movement jostles the man's sleeves, exposing the end of a thick black string. Adonis's eyes slowly follow where the twine leads and find it is woven into sutures identical to his, encircling both wrists.

It prompts a tsunami of emotion; he grits his teeth, and his jaw throbs from the pressure. The excruciating pain and horrific discovery compel him to desire death in its stead. He cannot comprehend why everything is happening to him, and tears fill his eyes as his quivering lips suppress a whimper.

Contradicting his suffering, the man joyfully swings his legs to the haunting rhythm of his tune. It angers Adonis and causes hatred to surge through his veins. His loathing is not just for the damage done but for the new grim reality of what he will never recover. Filled with a level of hatred he never thought possible, he tries not to upset his swollen jaw further, and he keeps his mouth closed to speak. "What did you do?" he asks; his words pierce the air.

The man continues to whistle happily, his tinny melody growing louder as he ignores him. Adonis cannot take the games any longer. Past the point of frustration, he releases a deep exhale through his nose, flaring his nostrils. "Answer me," he says. Irate, he breathes heavily, waiting for a response.

The whistling persists.

Realizing he is being ignored, he screams through his teeth. "I said answer me, goddammit!"

His captor halts his trill, stopping dead in his tracks.

Adonis is caught off-guard by the swift response, causing his eyes to widen as he frantically scans his surroundings for escape options.

Just a few steps away from them is the removed closet door. The sight of the splintered wood instantly triggers his dark thoughts, prompting his heart to race, and each heavy beat pounding against his chest wall ramps up his insanity.

In the absence of the stranger's haunting tune, the room's eerie silence emphasizes the houseboat's menacing nature.

Adonis reluctantly looks back at his captor. His stiffening body makes him appear taller than before. The sight of the dominant figure leaves him paralyzed with fear, tears streaming down his face as he struggles to catch his breath. "What have I done to make you hate me?" he asks. "Huh? What was it?"

His captor's body remains motionless.

Adonis snivels and refrains from looking away. His spiral of terror worsens. He talks faster, saying, "Did ... did I do something to you on the streets? Because if I did, you know I'm sorry. Out there, it's a dog-eat-dog world. Most of the time, I'm just trying to survive. We've all done shit we're not proud of, and it takes a man to admit that. I own up to my mistakes."

His captor, still facing forward, keeps holding onto his ankles silently, standing still.

Thinking he notices a slight sway in the man's shoulders, Adonis wants to keep his attention and swiftly continues. "But if I did ... this isn't how you settle a score. If you call it quits now, I promise to make it up to you for whatever happened."

The man gives his ankles a light squeeze.

Taking it as a sign, he is convinced he is getting through to the man and continues to plead for his life. "You know, I can tell what you are thinking. I know you're a good person, deep down. You have my word that I'll repay you two-fold. I'm telling you, man, I'm here to make things happen. Just give me the scoop on what you need. I got a guy for everything. Please ... leave me be. I don't know how much more of this my body can handle. The last thing we want is for either of us to have regrets. That shit will eat you alive."

The man clears his throat, and his voice deepens, taking on a darker tone. "Anything?" he asks.

Hearing the change in pitch makes Adonis second-guess himself. Even though he says he will do what he must, he questions the parameters of his offer, and before taking too much time for thought, he answers, "Well ... why don't you tell me what you have in mind first? Then we can discuss details." Anxiety and fear engulf him while he waits for a reply.

Abruptly, the man drops his ankles, and they hit the floor with a loud *thud*. Spinning his body around, he faces Adonis and responds with a silent glare; the moonlight reflects off the features of his face, illuminating his anger.

For the first time, he can clearly see the identity of his captor; it provokes a sinister reality that sweeps over him. "You...you..." he stammers. Grabbing the floor behind him, he drags himself backward.

Though wearing a different outfit, the same man had been haunting his reflection in the window—the one who had left burn marks on his shoulders and tried to suffocate him.

"It's ... you. But how..." Adonis says, trembling. He glances toward the window and, looking back at his captor, analyzes his expression.

His facial movements are unnatural; everything appears lagging and disjointed as if he is wearing a misfitted silicone mask. It adds an uncomfortableness as his closed-mouth grin stretches from ear to ear, and the bloodstained lighting from the nearby window casts a crimson reflection across his lips.

Matching each other's silence, they stare into one another's pupils. Adonis observes a lack of empathy in the man's gaze, and as he analyzes the dark circles more closely, his hope for survival fades as they reflect pure evil. "No, no, no," he says in a panic, scrambling backward to escape.

With a sinister smirk, the man does not say a word, and taking his time, he slowly approaches; each heavy footstep causes the end table next to the couch to rattle.

Adonis leaves his eyes fixed on him, paying no attention to his surroundings until his back collides with a piece of furniture.

Upon catching up, his captor looms over him, his face cold and expressionless. Without warning, he reaches down, snatches Adonis off the floor, and, cradling him in his arms, carries him toward the closet. As his limbs dangle helplessly, each movement causes sharp pain to radiate throughout his body. He wants to scream, but the agony in his jawbone forces him only to release a whimper.

The man pays him no attention as he continues to carry him; looking straight ahead, he grunts, heaving him into the closet.

As Adonis's body hits the floor, he lands on the pile of hangers. One of the wire hooks catches the center of his back with precise accuracy, tearing through his jacket and snaring the skin between his ribs. A surge of pain sweeps down his spine, turning his whimpering into a full-fledged wail. "Help me!" He screams at the top of his lungs.

Ignoring Adonis's screeches, the man advances toward the unhinged door. Picking it up by its splintered edges, he effortlessly shoves it back into the frame, forcing it to fit. The closet abruptly turns pitch black, filling the space with despair.

Adonis is overcome with agony, causing his eyesight to fade, and summoning all his energy, he unleashes a howl of pain. Rolling over, he faces the exit's direction, anticipating some response, but is met only with silence. The only sound filling his ears is the hangers crackling underneath him.

As he inhales slowly to take the edge off his agony, he is immediately stopped by a loud *thud* against the closet door. He flinches in surprise, driving the hanger deeper into his back and triggering painful spasms to scatter across his body.

The thunderous bang sounds again, resonating louder inside the small space.

He tries to stabilize his trembling hand as he reaches to his back and pulls the bloody metal hook from his flesh. Enraged, he throws it at the exit.

He can tell from the relentless pounding that someone is hammering from outside, and a sense of terror washes over him as he imagines being trapped alive. "Stop!" he shouts. "Please!"

Rather than slowing, the strikes continue at a faster pace.

The torment is unbearable. Lying motionless, he stares at the ceiling and cries; his claustrophobia triggers a wave of panic. "You're one sick bastard," he says with a growl. "There's a special place in hell for sickos like you."

The hammering immediately stops.

He quietly cries as he listens to the raspy breaths resonating from the other side of the door. The man's heavy footsteps slowly fade as he walks away.

In his abandonment, Adonis visualizes his two worst fears: dying and being alone when it happens. "Why?" He says, sniffling as he closes his eyes to pray. His crying causes his words to run together. "I mean ... I know I haven't made the most out of my life, but I swear I will turn it around if I make it out of here. I'm young ... I can't die now. I can't. I can still make something out of myself. Just give me a chance, okay? Please, God, for once in my life, listen to me."

Suddenly, the garments left on their hangers above sway, and the back-and-forth motion creates temporary circulation in the room's musty air. Unable to stomach the harsh sound of scratching metal any longer, Adonis winces through his agony to force his eyes open, and as he looks, he is hit with the remnants of a whisper lingering in the breeze. "Adonis..." it says.

As the sound trails off beneath the clothing, the garment's bright colors catch his eye. He finds their vibrant hues hypnotizing, standing out in the darkness.

With his attention captured, the voice speaks again, its gentle and alluring tone beckoning him closer. "Crawl," it says.

Its tone sends a shiver down his spine. Trying to follow its guidance, he works to move his legs, but everything feels numb. With no hope left, his lip quivers. "I ... I can't," he says.

Suddenly, several hangers shuffle beside him, clinking together; something is closing in.

Terrified and unable to see in the darkness, the unknown petrifies him. While he's refusing to look toward the rustling, a warm breath caresses the skin of his neck, and he feels the pressure of a body wrapping around him. His pain decreases, and the feeling returns to his limbs.

Gently, the voice softly whispers to him. "Do you trust me?" it asks, the words so close that he can almost feel them being spoken.

Adonis imagines them embracing his ears, filling him with a euphoric high, like morphine coursing through his veins. Assuming someone is finally answering his prayer, he is overwhelmed by the thought of being saved. "Are you an angel?" he asks. He takes a deep breath, giving in as the warmth infiltrates more of his being.

"Follow me," it says, now echoing from a short distance away, the whisper lingering beneath the hanging garments. Longing for it to continue, he closes his eyes and nods in compliance as a comforting warmth envelopes him.

The clothing gently sways, and the bustling noise makes way for a whisper. "Adonis..." the voice says, slowly trailing off behind the rack.

Leaving his eyes closed, he senses a force tugging at him, lifting his shoulders. The garments continue to stir, shifting faster to get his attention. "Under here," it says. Its quiet demeanor triggers an enigmatic pull.

He feels drawn to it and, sitting up, slowly opens his eyes. As he looks at the rack, he realizes his pain has disappeared, and, in disbelief, he pats the areas of his injuries; everything is okay.

The clothing hangers create a light scraping sound as they shift on the hanging rod. Still sensitive to noise, the sound alerts him, grabbing his attention. He wonders if it is the person who helped him. Squinting, he tries to see through the dark while nervously clearing his throat to speak. "Hell—hello?" he asks.

A single dress sways.

He gulps to clear a knot from his throat and, remaining cautious, moves closer to get a better look. "Is someone there?" he asks.

Whispers resonate from every corner of the closet, meeting at the room's center, swirling upward, encircling the light, and making it buzz. It catches his attention, and his eyes drift up to look. The lightbulb subtly flickers as it fights to come back to life.

His pupils dilate to match the building glow, and as the light settles in, he notices the bottom of the garments swishing. He tries to ignore it until he hears something scurrying.

A sudden *thud* from the back of the closet startles him. The abrupt noise triggers a bead of sweat to roll from his brow, and, taking a deep breath, he tilts his gaze toward the floor, ready to face whatever lurks there.

At first glance, there is no sign of anything. He appears to be alone.

An eeriness chills the room. Shivering, he lowers himself to the floor, and, on all fours, he looks underneath the dangling fabric.

There is only a lint ball perched in the corner.

Slowly, he crawls toward the hanging garments to get a closer look.

A woman's laugh echoes from beneath the clothes.

Caught by surprise, his eyes bulge, and he stops crawling. He cautiously looks ahead and calls out in a timid tone, "Is someone there?"

Instantly, the laughter dies, and the closet falls silent. The dramatic shift sends a rush of adrenaline through him. He takes another moment to listen for a response, then continues his approach. Little by little, he creeps closer, his palms drenched with sweat. They stick to the wooden floor, and he wipes them dry using one of the hanging dresses.

He peeks through the garments as the lightbulb emits the faintest of light.

The space is empty.

Seeing that the coast is clear, he crawls to the back of the closet through the dangling fabric and swivels to face the door's direction. After recognizing that his nerves have affected his breathing, he sits and rests his back against the wall to stabilize himself and catch his breath.

The quiet of the space brings peace. Feeling the extent of his fatigue, he releases a hefty sigh and, allowing his eyes to shut, leans more of his weight into the wall.

For the first time, he feels safe.

Ten

LEAVE YOUR EYES CLOSED

As Adonis drifts into a deep sleep, daylight stirs outside. The remaining birds rise, and what should be happy chirps are now cries from the ravenous beaks of vultures. Swooping down, they dive from the sky, pecking flesh from the carcasses decomposing on the deck.

Dreaming of nothing, his mind sees a blank canvas of black, allowing him to rest; it's his intuition's way of protecting him from the terror of something lurking.

On the other side of the wall, behind his head, are a pair of fingers. The nails move unhurriedly from top to bottom, lightly scratching the wood, the delicate motion adding to the ambiance resembling a trickle of water.

Incoherently, Adonis emerges from his deep sleep and shifts his head, not knowing why he has been disrupted.

Half-awake, he mumbles a few disjointed words before drifting back into a deeper slumber, this time snoring.

The thing that awaits on the opposite side of the wall stops scraping and places its ear against the wood to listen. After carefully processing the noise produced by his body's twitches, it resumes its taunting, shifting its fingers' approach to tap the wood. "Wake up," it says; its voice is barely audible. The muffled words are timed with the *rata tat tat* against the paneling as it chants, "Wake up...wake up...wake up."

As the sound of the pecking migrates across the wall, it lands near Adonis's head and enters his ear, infiltrating his dreamless state and gnawing at his attention. His eyes flutter open. Groggy and in a state of confusion, he tries to process his surroundings. His heart races as he realizes he is on the opposite side of the clothing rack and cannot recall how he got there. Giving himself a moment, he leans forward and peers beneath the dangling clothes, focusing on the bottom of the door.

The daylight from the living room squeezes through the tiny crack and infiltrates inside, illuminating the closet's chaotic state. He rubs his eyes and yawns. His gaze scans everywhere the light touches, and everything appears to be in the same chaotic state he left it.

The hangers still rest in a pile, a bloody luster staining several wire hooks.

As he recollects the horror, the thought of one clawing at his skin makes him sweat, and, overcome with panic, he quickly feels for the injury to his spine. "Don't be real ... please, please be my imagination," he says. Finding no sign of injury, he exhales a sigh of relief and, glancing at the ceiling, nervously laughs. "Thank you, Jesus."

The finger taps against the wall behind him, creating the background noise.

His posture stiffens mid-chuckle, and he falls silent as his eyes anxiously scan the room. "Is ... is someone there?" he asks. Clearing his throat, he sits up taller in a show of dominance and lowers his voice to a more threatening tone. "If someone is, you better reveal yourself now, or else."

Nothing but silence fills the air.

Still unable to trust the peace, Adonis gives himself another moment to listen. As he tries to remain patient, he sits in uncomfortable anticipation, waiting for the other shoe to drop.

Seconds turn to minutes in the room's continued stagnancy.

The unwavering calm floods him with a sense of relief, and, letting his guard down, his shoulders relax and his body slumps. "Boy, oh, boy," he says, shaking his head. "I have to stop being so—"

A loud crash against the wall cuts off his speech.

It paves the way for a barrage of frantic knocks. The frantic pounding implies that something is trapped and desperately trying to escape.

His pupils dilate, and fear keeps his words trapped behind his lips. The piercing blows cause his mind to recall the image of the birds' blood spattering the living room window. Terrified, he spins around to face the direction of the noise while kicking his legs against the floor to scoot himself away. The racked clothing brushes against his back, making him jump as he hyper-focuses on the wood-paneled wall.

Every second that passes, the number of deafening knocks increases, spreading to the four walls around him. Overwhelmed by the chaos, his mind shuts down, and he rocks back and forth. The noise eats away at his psyche, leaving his brain ready to explode, and, on the verge of an outburst, he cannot hold in his emotions any longer. "What the hell do you want from me?" he shouts.

Abruptly, the room falls silent.

He tightens his hug around his knees. Incessant ringing haunts his ears, and he closes his eyes, quickening his rocking to calm himself. "See? It's all in your head," he says.

A voice calls to him, wanting him to open his eyes. "Adonis," it says.

He can tell by its muffled sound that it is coming from the other side of the wall. Trying to ignore it, he shakes his head. "Nope," he says. "We are not doing that."

"Adonis," it says again, with more conviction.

Hearing his name causes his body to tremble and his breathing to become labored as he fights the urge to comply.

The whisper calls out again, urging him to listen. "Adonis," it says.

Although he wants to disregard it, he finds that the more he denies it, the louder it becomes, and reluctantly, seeing no other option, he lifts his eyes to look.

Suddenly, a wooden panel on the wall creaks. He is horrified as he watches, unable to look away, as it wiggles slightly, creating small gaps around the edges. Goosebumps cover him at the thought of what could lurk on the other side.

"In here. Hurry," it says. The voice stemming from the slits seems anxious; its tempo is choppy and disjointed.

At once, the timbre makes him reflect on the person who had healed him. He cannot help comparing them; both voices sound the same. The similarity brings a wave of guilt over him for her suffering, and he knows that since she helped him, he must do something. He takes a deep breath and blinks to confirm that what he sees is real before speaking. "Excuse me?" He asks, hoping it will go away. He waits for a response.

Rather than disappearing, it stays put, silent.

He tries swallowing his fear while carefully shifting his body forward and peering into the dark hole. "Are... are you trapped?" he asks. His stammer worsens as he continues, "Just... um... give me a sign if you need help."

The board frantically vibrates.

Not expecting a sign, he nervously jumps and stumbles to his knees. Ignoring his instincts, he picks himself up and carries on with another attempt. "Okay, just hold on. Don't worry, I'll get you out," he says. He briefly pauses, taking a moment to gather his confidence.

Motionless, the unwavering shadow watches him.

He reaches for the board and, grabbing hold, pulls with all his might, freeing one side. Then, with a final yank, he removes it from the wall.

Beyond the new opening, everything appears darker than expected; shapes and outlines blend into the hopeless abyss.

He clears the phlegm from his throat. "Hello?" he says.

A scurrying noise sounds from inside the darkness, gradually receding further into the void before ceasing. "Please help me," it says.

Adonis is left puzzled as he continues to grasp the piece of wood, wondering why the voice retreated. "Can you move a little closer?" he asks, squinting to get a better look.

Without hesitation, it answers. "I can't. I think I'm stuck," it says, but unlike before, the tone lacks emotion.

Beads of sweat form on Adonis's forehead as he struggles with uncertainty over what to do; the mere thought of entering the dark, unfamiliar room fills him with panic.

The voice timidly whimpers, "Please, I'm afraid."

Even though something feels off, the helpless tone tugs at his heartstrings. The stress causes an ache in his upper back, prompting him to shrug his shoulders and shake off his nerves. "Ok. I'm coming. Just stand back and hang in there," he says.

With a split-second decision, he erratically begins tearing the adjacent boards from the wall. As more are removed, the air from the hidden space infiltrates the closet; the temperature is ice cold. Shivering, he removes the last board and, feeling winded by the effort, takes a moment to catch his breath.

Ready to confront the unknown, he scans the darkness. There is a slight shuffling emanating from the furthest corner. "Over here," it says.

It sends a chill down his spine, causing his limbs to freeze. He is irritated by his lack of control and quickly tries to shake it off. "Come on, you got to man up," he says.

Wooden boards are scattered across the ground surrounding him. He carefully lowers himself onto his hands and knees, pushes the debris aside, and crawls forward, inching his way inside. Feeling the floor for guidance, he creeps further into the lightless space. "See? It's not so bad. Nothing to worry about," he says with a nervous chuckle. "It's like strolling down main street at night."

A sudden gust of wind brushes past him as he advances.

Without warning, the pitter-patter of footsteps, followed by a high-pitched cackle, breaks through the silence.

Stricken with terror, a tremble rolls through his body, almost knocking him over; he feels his arms give out underneath him. "Just the wind," he says. "That's all it is." Despite his attempt to downplay the situation, his body's tremors escalate, making it impossible to ignore the truth.

Again, the room becomes silent, but only for a second; clinking metal rings through the air, and the sound of shackles hitting the wooden floorboards cuts through the stagnant cold.

The noise paralyzes him. His mind flashes back to waking up chained to the bed; he feels like he cannot move, trapped in his anxiety. As his pupils expand, consuming the bulk of his irises, he appears to have seen a ghost. Entombed in chaos, everything feels as if it is spinning around him.

Again, metal clanks against the floor.

He wants to exit the room but knows he cannot leave without the person who saved his life. His speech quickens, and his voice lowers to a forceful whisper. "Give me a sign or something," he says, scanning the darkness.

Abruptly, a chain slams to the ground as if demanding to be heard. He tentatively turns toward the piercing sound. It is coming from the far-right corner of the room.

A rigid lump forms in his throat, and he realizes that if he waits any longer, fear may overpower him. He grits his teeth, determined to push through.

Unable to see any walls, the dark abyss presents an illusion; there is no way to tell the distance. As he crawls carefully toward the noise, the further he gets from his original point of entry, the less convinced he becomes that there is an end.

Just as he is about to turn around, his palm lands on a piece of icy metal, sending a shiver up his arm. Upon grasping it, he instantly knows he has discovered the chain.

A soft whimper rings through the obscurity. It is coming from the end of the chain.

With a firm grip on the cold metal, he strains his eyes to see through the darkness, his narrowed gaze fixed on what he hopes is a short distance ahead. Using the chain as a guide, he pulls himself closer hand over hand, heedlessly allowing it to lead him toward completing his mission. "Almost there ... just a few more steps... just a little further," he says, his voice filled with cautious determination.

The closer the chain's end becomes, the colder the temperature gets. Each handful of links sticks to his palms, almost pulling off the skin.

While grabbing the next handful of the chain, he realizes he has reached the end and found the shackle. He scrambles to locate the person's ankle to help free them, and, in his frenzy, he overshoots his target, face-planting against the wooden floor.

He picks himself up and frantically searches for the shackle, only to find the heavy loop empty. "But...but...

where..." he says, stammering; his face turns pale, and his eyes dart through the darkness.

The closet light flickers.

His focus shifts to the hole in the wall; it looks miles away. "Shit," he says. While fixating on the light in the distance, a high-pitched scream grabs his attention, cutting off his train of thought.

He watches the flickering light in the closet, straining to see or hear any hint of where the distressed person might be hiding. Abruptly, the closet door swings open, allowing the light from the living room to flood inside, infiltrating the hidden chamber.

Initially, he looks at it with confusion without considering the cause. It makes little sense to him. He vividly remembers the door being nailed shut by his captor, but before he can overthink it, he is drawn to the light permeating the surrounding space.

Never having seen the area illuminated before, he uses it to his advantage to investigate. Anticipating seeing something resembling a storage room, he expects nothing unusual. He takes a deep breath and, beginning at the furthest corner, scans from floor to ceiling.

The surrounding space is ample and roughly the same size as a typical bedroom. As he moves his gaze to the wall, he realizes that there are oddly no windows, making the room appear like a dungeon.

While Adonis analyzes the space, his attention is suddenly diverted upon hearing struggling sounds from the living room. "What the..." he says. As he starts his sentence, ready to investigate, he stops. Something catches his eye nearby.

A chain is bolted down to where the wall intersects with the wooden floor. It is identical to the one in his hand. His intestines churn, and nausea sets in as his eyes are drawn to a disturbing sight farther into the room.

Equally spaced down the wall are more restraints. Each is engulfed in rust and bolted to the floor. The only difference between them is the discolored wood underneath. Each board is flushed with a blackened burgundy hue, with some darker than others, depending on age.

As he connects the dots of the gruesome scene, his imagination runs wild. As he holds the shackle in his hand, horror washes over him. Dropping the heavy restraint, he scrambles to escape while trying not to scream upon seeing a trail of blood staining the wood he is kneeling on. The red's brightness shows it is fresher than the rest.

Unable to control his hyperventilation, the skin on the back of his neck becomes prickly, and warmth trickles across his hairline. Feeling something watching him, his fear plunges him into paralysis. He winces and reluctantly shifts his eyes, unable to ignore the irking sensation.

Looking from his peripherals, he glimpses something to the side of him: human skeletal remains lie in the room's corner, partially propped up, the sockets of its eye bones angled upward, staring at him. Its broken jaw leaves its mouth gaped open.

The sight of its mummified skin and brittle hair makes his knees give out underneath him. "No, no, no, no," he says anxiously. Trying to scurry away, he feels trapped as his back hits the wall. The image keeps replaying in his head, no matter how hard he tries to dismiss it.

Abruptly, a woman's bloodcurdling scream adds to the horrific ambiance.

Amid his frantic confusion, he stands frozen in place, unsure of what to do, his gaze fixated on the noise's direction. As he takes a moment to process what is happening, his ears are assaulted by a loud *thud* and the sound of something being dragged across the floor. His stomach drops at the sound of the chaotic struggle, and he glances toward the noise.

As his vision lands on the closet, he notices something is different: all the clothes once piled on the floor no longer scatter the ground; the heap has been rehung on the rack and is perfectly organized. It makes him second-guess his recollection of the trauma he had endured and his reality.

With his brow furrowed in deep thought, a single bead of sweat trickles down into his eye, stinging it. Worried he is losing time, he cannot wrap his head around what he sees, and things spiral out of control before he can decipher it.

The screaming resumes, and the door to the closet opens wider.

With only the shadow of legs visible under the dress's hems, he recognizes the movement and silhouette—it is the fishing waders of his captor. Overwhelmed with terror, goosebumps form on his body, and holding his breath, he moves his head toward the floor to continue watching.

Facing the door to the living room, the man bends down to adjust his grip on something.

Almost at the level of his eyes, Adonis notices a pair of heels draped over his forearms; clearly, he is dragging a woman's body. He fights back a gasp and covers his mouth with his hands.

As the man adjusts his grip on her ankles, he gives her body a pull, yanking her inside. The noise of the closet door slamming shut triggers the woman to stir awake. "What ... what are you doing?" she asks as she looks at him through bleary eyes, appearing to be under a drug's influence. "Where am I?"

He ignores her questions while undressing her. She tries to fight back, but her incoherent state renders her powerless as she flails her hands to resist him. After finishing, he disregards her; holding her dress gently in his grasp, he takes a deep smell of the lace on the sleeves. "A nice thing like you doesn't deserve to be on a woman like that." He says.

She is lying on the ground, completely naked, shivering. Embarrassed and hazy, she tries to move, but she feels her body going numb. In a panic, she paws at her knees. "I can't feel my legs, " she says, her unnerving screams growing louder. "What did you do to me?"

Happily coddling the dress, he whistles and, blocking out her cries, finds an empty hanger on the rack. With a smirk, he carefully hangs the garments up. "There we are," he says. "Welcome to your new home." Watching the dress sway on the rack, he sighs, then flips through the others, admiring his collection.

Her arms claw toward the walls as more of her body becomes numb. "Please, someone help," she says, "Anyone ... please, he's going to kill..."

In a swooping motion, he turns around to face her and plucks her up by her hair. "It's time to go," he says.

The violent jerking motion of her head causes her neck to snap.

Adonis watches in horror as her head falls forward, hanging flaccidly. Even though he wants to help, he is worried about being next, and knowing his life will be jeopardized if he is found, he scans the windowless room for a place to hide.

With Adonis's back turned, his captor slowly parts the blazers and dresses on the rack, creating a small opening with his fingers.

Panic sets in as he realizes the room lacks any furniture that could serve as a hiding spot, leaving him trembling as he faces the only item in the space: the mummified corpse. With no other options, he synchronizes each movement to the piercing sound of the hangers scraping against the metal rod as he slowly inches toward it in the room's corner.

The man shuffles the garments, producing a considerable space between them, then trudges through the gap and proceeds into the hidden room. He drags the woman behind him with callous intent, causing her flesh to scrape against the floorboard's ridges.

Adonis frantically wiggles to hide beneath the desiccated corpse and, peeking through a puncture wound in its ribcage, watches the man's leisurely approach. As his whistling tune echoes between the walls, each note is accented by the woman's gurgling lungs expelling pink fluid. The floor creaks beneath his heavy steps as he moves to each chain, checking the fit of every shackle around her neck.

Adonis watches in horror as he chooses the chain he had recently held in his grasp. Terrified of the man's proximity, he remains still and takes shallow breaths to avoid being detected. He wraps his hands around the corpse's arms to shield himself, feeling the roughness of the mummified skin beneath his quivering fingertips.

The stench of decayed flesh under his nose makes him grimace as he watches the man chain the woman to the floor. The man smiles, looking at her.

Adonis tightly closes his eyes to wipe the image from his mind and, not hearing any movement, waits a moment to listen.

Everything is eerily quiet.

Unsure of what he may discover, he gulps air and opens his eyes.

Again, he finds nothing as he had remembered. His hands, still clenched, are empty. The corpse he had relied on for protection is gone. Stricken with fear, his wide eyes look at the shackles on the floor in front of him.

Aside from the chains, the one thing that remains constant is the severely injured woman's presence.

His anxiety races as he scans the space, and, not seeing any sign of the man, he looks toward the closet.

The woman's finger gives a slight twitch.

Adonis is taken aback by her survival and tries to get her attention. "Hey ... hey," he says in a trembling whisper. Seeing no response, he rushes toward her helpless body.

She lies naked on the floor, her wrists and ankles bearing deep lacerations from days of struggling to break free from the iron restraints. Her eyes bulge as she gasps for air, her lips slowly turning purple from oxygen deprivation.

Trying to help, he desperately pulls at the metal collar around her neck.

A tear rolls down her cheek as she looks at him with a gape of terror he has never seen before—the tendons of her neck tense as her restrained limbs try to move. In a fit of fear, she tries to fight him off. "No ... please," she says; her constricted airway makes her voice difficult to hear.

Struggling to free the shackle, his fingers tremble. "It's okay ... you are just a little confused. I'm trying to help," he says, looking into her eyes.

He stops. There is something familiar about her; he has seen her before. Even though he tries not to put too much thought behind it, her face strikes a nerve within him, and he cannot stop his mind from wandering.

Slowly, her breathing weakens.

He feels trapped in his head. As he digs deeper into his memories, he recalls a time when he would panhandle outside a beignet shop just a short distance from his hometown. A specific recollection floods back to him as he thinks of the cold early morning hours. He remembers her passing by him often while on her way to work. She always seemed to be on a mission to get inside, but even in a hurry, her cheerful face remained steadfast, etched into his mind. She was one of the few people who would take a moment to smile at him. Regardless of his unwillingness to reciprocate the kind gesture, it made him feel seen.

Her cough startles him, drawing him back from his thoughts and making his heart skip a beat. As he stares at her late teen face, her soft brown eyes confirm it is the same person. "But why would she be here..."

She struggles to take one last breath before her body falls limply silent.

In denial, he holds her head and gazes into her lifeless pupils. Even though he never knew her on a personal level, seeing someone die overwhelms him, and he fights back his tears. "Why? Why is he doing this?" He asks. "What made him do that to her?" Grief-stricken, he battles to find his voice and remain calm.

Something rustles in the distance, setting him on edge.

Skittishly, he glances toward the closet and, becoming distracted, is complacent about what is happening before him—her body's transformation to a mummified state. The sudden coldness on her skin makes him look down, and his eyes widen with terror upon realizing he is now holding the skull of the corpse he had hidden behind in the room's corner. "Get ... get the hell off me!" he shouts; he swiftly shoves the body off his lap.

Upon her lifeless shell hitting the unforgiving floor, her brittle skin cracks like porcelain, and the impact deepens the fracture in her neck and shatters one of her shoulder blades into dust. Screaming, Adonis frantically pushes against the floor to distance himself from the carcass as his breaths become shorter and dizziness consumes him. His eyes hyper-focus on the crumbling shoulder, he clutches his chest, and his face turns pale.

As he looks on in horror, a loud crackle emanates from the neck as the decrepit head turns. It comes to a stop, staring directly at him.

He rubs his eyes, desperately wanting it to stop, thinking his mind is playing tricks on him. As the unrelenting horror persists, he cannot decipher what is real and what is not. His teeth chatter, and his heart races as the body's raspy voice fills the air with a moan.

The woman's bony fingers make a jarring movement as they lift and grasp the sides of her neck. Their death grip tightens, and her nails lock around the brittle cartilage. The bone crumbles from the pressure of her digits, causing her neck to snap and freeing her from the entrapment of the shackle.

The resounding crack of the head breaking free and the clinking of the metal hitting the floor make Adonis flinch, his eyes fixated as both wobble several times before settling. Abruptly, his focus is seized by the movement of her lower limbs gathering beneath her.

Now freed from her confines, she rises to her feet.

Terrified of the body's reanimation and uncertain of what will happen next, Adonis nervously scans the room for a way of escape or a place to hide.

The head eerily follows his movement and mimics his squirming. "You," she says, hissing. "You did this to me." As the buzz from her tongue lingers, her desiccated eyes shift in their sockets, tracking him. Her brow bone lifts, creating a bridge of curiosity as she fixates on his growing anxiety.

He tries to maintain composure as his gawping gaze darts the room, but his nerves get the best of him, causing him to word vomit his defense. "What? No. Me? I ... I don't know you like that. We've never even talked before. "I think you've got the wrong guy," he says, stumbling over his words. He frantically digs his heels into the floorboards as he scrambles backward to escape.

She tracks him while her mouth signals her disjointed body to join in the hunt with a click of her tongue. Her parched lips twitch to form an ominous grin. "Get him," she says with a voice that is clear as day.

Immediately, her rigid legs react to her words, releasing resounding cracks. Like the start-up of a machine, their uncoordinated movements slowly come together, causing the headless carcass to take its first steps.

The sight of the decapitated figure walking toward him incites panic, and, terrified, he clambers to stand. With fear gripping him, he redirects his attention toward the dimly lit closet, weighing his options. Unsure of what to do next and struggling to decide, he refocuses on the approaching corpse as he desperately makes one last attempt to make peace. "I didn't come here to stir up trouble," he says. He refrains from glancing behind him while slowly backing away.

Savoring the room's building anticipation, the woman's mouth opens, giving an intentional pause before speaking. Drawn to the movement, his gaze fixates on the mummified tongue. It wiggles like an earthworm as she wheezes, and then, shifting tones, she demonically cackles. "Run," she says.

Awaiting her command, the mummified legs alter positions and, in a split second, aggressively take off in a sprint.

The sound of the flat feet triggers a wave of adrenaline in Adonis; he does not have to look at them to know they are headed in his direction. Listening to his instincts, he turns toward the closet and runs.

From all sides of the room, the chains bolted to the floor clink and clank, thrashing against the steel shackles, their menacing chaos heckling him to flee in terror. The closer he gets to the closet, the louder the bare feet slap behind him. His vision tunnels as he focuses solely on staying alive.

Chanting voices fill the air, calling for him. "Adonis, Adonis," they say, "Over here ... over here!" Although their pitch and tone differ, each plagues his ears with obscene darkness, coaxing him to stay.

"Come on, focus," he says. His neck aches as he fights the urge to turn toward their pull, determined to keep looking straight ahead as he tries to escape. Vocalizing his resistance, he shouts at the top of his lungs, "I'm not falling for your tricks!"

They hiss, feeding off his disdain. As their anger escalates, so does the volume and intensity of their speech. "Stay!" they shout.

Covered in sweat, Adonis senses warm air coming from the closet, enticing him to step closer and cross the breached wall.

The voices scream louder in his ears.

In his desperate attempt to flee the chaos, he stumbles, tripping on the uneven floor. His arms swing wildly as if attempting to grab the air to steady himself, and, unsuccessful, he tumbles to his knees.

Abruptly, the heckling stops.

He takes a moment to catch his breath; the eerie calmness sends a jitter down his spine. Now face to face with the hanging garments once more, he squints to adjust to the closet's lighting as his fists clenched, ready to fight. Fueled by anger, he lets out a deep growl, whirls around, and charges toward the concealed room on his knees.

As he speeds toward the wall, he is met with a face full of wood. The hole he had created is gone.

As his ears ring from the impact, he clutches his bruised nose and sits in confusion, looking at the barrier. Ignoring his throbbing head, he slowly crawls forward, then places his hands flat against the wooden paneling.

The wall is cold to the touch. He shivers as he recalls the room's frigid temperature and, unable to sort through the realities, is concerned that he may go insane. With a strong desire for answers, he nervously taps the wall with his trembling hand.

Everything is quiet. It is just as he expected, and shaking his head, he chuckles. "Adonis, guess what? You're something else. You're worse than those cats on the street—the ones that talk to themselves."

Just when he is about to relax, he is startled by three faint knocks from the partitioned room on the other side of the wall.

Immediately, his throat tightens, and his stomach drops. "It ... it was real," he says in a state of shock, his eyes widened in terror. "That—that thing was real." Frantically, he scurries away from the wall, his back colliding with the hanging clothes, making them sway.

The feeble light flickers overhead.

Eleven

HIDDEN UNDERNEATH

Taking a deep breath, Adonis peers under the clothing toward the door. Unsure of what to expect, he is surprised to see that it is shut. He vividly remembers seeing it open through the darkness of the hidden space.

The more he focuses on it, the more unsettled he becomes upon noticing something he missed earlier: deep gashes etched into the bottom of the door. The indentations are still visible despite having been filled and covered with paint.

Adonis remembers the sound of the woman clawing to get away from the man after he stripped her naked; her screams repeat in his mind.

It is not just one set of scratch marks; layers of disfigurement mar the wood. The damage is from years of constant abuse and serves as a haunting reminder of the cruelty that had occurred there.

"That couldn't have been there before," he says. "I would have remembered it." The more he thinks about it, the more the woman's struggle haunts him, and, wanting to avoid the memory, his attention shifts, fixating on the lock.

He initially believed the door was nailed shut, but after watching it open and close in the darkness, he realized his safety was an illusion. He is at the end of his patience; his spiraling mind and fear-driven actions have left him exhausted and irritable. As he recollects everything he has seen, he realizes he has enough evidence against his captor to force his compliance, and he prepares to speak, ready to regain his freedom.

On cue, the light above gives three quick flickers. The disruption abruptly derails his train of thought and redirects his attention toward the fixture.

His eyes are immediately drawn to a fly buzzing around the lightbulb, its ample size making it impossible to ignore. As it lands on the glass, an electrical shock surges through its body, causing it to tumble toward the floor. Gracefully touching down on its back, it settles near the rack, and its thin legs give one last wiggle before it dies.

Taking it as an omen of his impending fate, he works quickly to craft a threat against his captor. He lowers his belly to the floor so his voice will project into the living room. "I know what you did," he says, trembling. He feels fulfilled by his strong start and is pleased with his approach. His voice gains power, becoming more assertive with every sentence. "You hear me? I found out your dirty little secret. You might think you can hide shit from me, but you can't. And here's something you don't know: I've been playing you all along, not the other way around!"

He feels a new sense of confidence and continues despite not having a clear plan. "Yup. That's right ... I don't live on the street...Actually, I'm an undercover cop ... and about ready to bust your ass."

Everything remains quiet.

As he revels in his cockiness, he closes one eye to focus on the narrow view beneath the doorframe, watching for any sign of movement. "How does that feel? Huh? I bet you didn't see this plot twist coming," he says, imagining his captor buying into his fraudulent storyline.

Even though he finds the image satisfying, he wants tangible proof of the man's reaction to his revenge scheme. Wanting to see him squirm, he slinks out from underneath the clothes and positions himself closer to the door to get a better view.

Timed with his movement, the light flickers overhead, and combined with the residue left by the insect's electrocution on the bulb, it casts an ominous bullseye on his back.

He talks faster as he continues unloading more threats, his overconfidence blinding him to the lurking danger. "Yeah, I bet you are sweating right now. You know what I found? Your creepy room and the stash of matchboxes. Not just that.... I saw the dresses. If you let me go right now, no one needs to find out about your little hobby. This is what we call a fair trade, my friend. Just give me a yes, and we're good to go. No one will ever find out - it'll be our little secret."

The same as before, he is met with silence.

Adonis laughs sarcastically, convinced he has his captor exactly where he wants him.

Simultaneously, the handle of the closet door gently turns, and without a sound, the entrance creeps open a sliver.

He is oblivious to the activity as he replays the critical points of his speech. "Man, that was good," he says, whispering. The only thing on his mind is whether there's more he wants to say.

Since he's been on the houseboat, his memory has become fragmented like a patchwork quilt, leaving him uncertain about the accuracy of his accusations. He is relying on his vague statements to help him get what he wants. His experience on the streets has made him well-versed in leverage, and if there is one thing he has learned over the years, it is that people will eventually fold if their reputation is at stake.

The door opens further, swinging toward him and making him flinch. He takes a step back. A screech sounds from the hinges, and the late-morning light funnels in through the crack. "I knew he'd come to his senses," he says with a smirk. "Looks like someone is finally ready to talk."

He squints to adjust his eyes to the bright, inviting gleam. "It's about time we end this bullshit," he says. Feeling that he has the upper hand, he takes a deep breath in anticipation of his victory.

A subtle whisper lingers behind him, producing a puff of air that tousles his hair. Ignoring it, he brushes it off and confidently grabs the doorknob. "Nothing is going to dampen my shine. I knew we would come to an understanding eventually. I just knew it," he says, giving the handle a stern tug.

As he peers into the newly exposed space, he finds the room empty. The moment unfolds differently from what he had imagined. Instead of facing his captor, he stands there, staring blankly, trying to make sense of the situation.

Like several times before, everything appears to have been neatly reset. Yet again, he feels duped. He wants to scream but stops when he hears something rustling in the kitchen.

The sound is reminiscent of a hack saw's long strokes against a thick branch. He tries to remain calm, but the noise is unbearable. The tension in his jaw causes it to twitch, and the longer he waits for the man to come forward, the angrier he gets. Gritting his teeth, he steps out of the closet, slamming the door behind him. "Face me like a man, you coward!" he shouts.

The situation is wreaking havoc on his mental state. He's reached his breaking point. In a fit of rage, he directs his glare toward the kitchen.

A gangly man donning fishing attire stoops over the sink, whistling. Recognizing him as his captor, Adonis yells loudly, ensuring anyone within a five-mile radius can hear. "If you want to play this game, we can play this game, you son of a bitch!" he shouts, storming the room.

The man continues to ignore him as he works away.

Each of Adonis's footsteps causes the floor's aged structure to rattle; its vibration is consistent with a minor earthquake.

The lack of response triggers him further, and, even though on a mission, he quiets his approach and listens closer; something about the man's activity rattles his gut as sounds of splashing and sawing resound from the kitchen sink.

The noise is jarring.

Adonis carefully moves closer, his heart racing as he peers to see what he is doing. However, he soon regrets succumbing to his curiosity.

Partially submerged in the sink's pink, soapy water is a woman's headless torso. As the man takes a break from sawing, he places the hacksaw beneath his arm and, grabbing a sponge from the water, begins scrubbing her coco flesh. "Men like girls who wash," he says.

Adonis watches in horror as he places the corpse's hand on the counter and saws through the bone with a disturbing level of precision. "Gator bites," he says, "Just a few more to go. Now we just gotta wrap you up and throw you in the freezer before you spoil."

Adonis ducks low to the floor as his captor turns with the severed part in hand. He watches him methodically wrap the limb layer after layer of garbage sacks and brown shipping tape.

Once done, the man whistles as he scans the shelves in the freezer for the perfect spot.

Then, like a butcher organizing their meat locker, he shuffles the packages to make space for the limb.

Adonis struggles to maintain his composure while waiting for him to refocus on the sink. As soon as he sees his attention diverted, he pivots, scanning the hallway for an escape route. Noticing that the bedroom door is partially open, he slowly crawls toward it.

The man freezes in place, dropping the saw onto the floor.

Adonis hears the metal hitting the ground and, springing to his feet, braces himself for a confrontation. But the man has vanished.

His unpredictability causes Adonis to snap, and succumbing to his rage, he kicks anything in his way.

"I'm gonna find you," he says, each angry word spewing spit. "And when I do...you'll wish you never fucked with my life."

Having lost all patience, he takes out his frustration on the partially opened bedroom door, delivering a powerful kick that shatters the fragile wood and leaves behind a mark of destruction. Its momentum produces an ear-shattering crash as it collides with the room's wall.

Out of breath from his outburst, he steps inside the space, intending revenge. He scans the room, looking for the man.

At first glance, the bedroom looks identical to how he remembers it, except for the absence of dust and cobwebs. Then he observes that despite the bed remaining disheveled, the sheets have been substituted with immaculate white ones.

He immediately races over and feels the top of the mattress. It is warm to the touch. The surface's elevated temperature is all the evidence he needs to know that it has just been slept on. He clutches the sheets and, tightening his grip, rips them from the bed. "You're not fooling anyone! I know you've been here!" He shouts, his words echoing between the walls.

Taking a moment, he notices something disgusting on the bare mattress: there is a large dark stain embedded deeply in the fibers.

Trying to control his nausea, he wonders if it is blood. The thought is unsettling to his nerves, and he slowly backs away.

A noise resonates from under the bed; something rustles against the carpet. His attention darts to the shadowy, confined space, and, petrified, his hand drops the bedsheet to the floor. As the thing stirs below, the sound becomes more distinct, resembling a set of fingernails scratching the underside of the frame. The grating sound messes with his mind, and he cannot help but wonder who is causing it. Thinking it may be his captor, he pushes back his sleeves, ready to fight, but upon taking his first step, he hears a sound that makes him freeze.

It is a woman's whisper. "Join us," she says. The melodic air of her words accents another scratch that digs deeper into the underside of the wooden frame.

His terror escalates, rendering him unable to speak more than one word. "No..." he says. Barely able to comprehend the turn of events, he glances at the closet and then back to the bed.

Abruptly, the floorboards creak behind him. The unsettling sound is instantly succeeded by a loud thump, causing him to startle and jump. With his confidence fading, he redirects his attention from the bed to what lies behind him.

Unlike how he had left it, the bedroom door is now closed. A shock wave travels through his body, fearing he may be trapped again. Even though he wonders if it is locked, he cannot bring himself to move his feet to check its status.

A loud *thud* resonates from beneath the bedframe, accompanied by more rustling against the carpet.

He swiftly pivots and pauses midway to monitor both disruptions, using his peripheral vision to detect any lurking presence. Abruptly, the scratching nails stop, and a faint sound emerges from the edge of the bed frame. Gripped by the sound, Adonis falls silent.

As he watches a single finger emerge from the dark abyss, he finds that the further it extends into the room, the harder it is to look away.

The skeletal structure of the hand is lanky and appears monstrous, with each of its nails jagged and discolored. The thin frame is comparable to the size of a large adult's hand.

Terror consumes him, and he wants to call for help, but knowing that no one will respond, he fears it is useless.

The finger leisurely shifts, taking its time to redirect its sharp tip toward the closet. As it flips over, it coils, wrapping around the wooden slats and securing its grip near the mattress's edge. The voice bellows incomprehensibly before slowly forming intelligible words. "Don't be afraid," she says. Her voice becomes graver with every word, and her diction cuts through the air like a snake's hiss. With a raspy breath, she whispers, "Only the brave choose to die. Death can be much less painful than life."

Her words send shivers down his spine. He thought he had solved the mystery of the houseboat and his mission was done, but the sinister presence makes him rethink his confidence. "Who ... are you?" he timidly asks while his eyes dart around, trying to plan an escape.

The creature's grip tightens around the edge of the bed, exposing more of its hand and turning its naturally dark ebony knuckles stark white under pressure, causing its purple veins to protrude. "You mean, who are we?" she says, correcting him. Her tone differs from before. Rather than singular, it resonates like a choir, projecting across multiple octaves. He cannot wrap his head around what she just said. Her statement leaves him unsure of what to do next.

"We?" He says.

Suddenly, a line of decaying hands burst from the darkness, their fingers coiling around the furniture like deadly vines. The sight of the zombie-like state of their skin makes his stomach churn.

"There can't be more," he says, his voice filled with disbelief as a glazed stare conceals his tearful eyes.

Suddenly, a rancid fog invades the room like a gas chamber, carrying the smell of death. With every breath he takes, the pungent air attacks his lungs, leaving him unable to stop coughing.

As chaos swirls around him, the monstrous hands clutch tighter onto the bedframe, wanting to free themselves; their pulling force causes the heavy wooden bed to slide. The wooden legs lift from the ground, revealing the naked, partially decomposed bodies belonging to the hands.

Their rotting flesh holds Adonis's attention, the peeling layers revealing the discolored tendons and muscles that cling to their bones. He whimpers as he hastily surveys each face in panic, seeking their identities, but, like the corpse from the closet, their facial features are concealed behind embryo-like masks of thin skin.

The similarity triggers a horrid memory of the woman climbing onto him, and he hyperventilates. As his eyes continue scanning the frail bodies, his attention lands on the one furthest away; there is something different about it. Even though its flesh has been rotted away and its genitalia removed, he notices the muscle structure. Its broad shoulders and taller stance appear masculine; the build is not of a female like to others, but a male.

Finding the stark difference odd, he takes a split second to scan its body. There are fewer rotted pieces and discoloration marks; the man's frame looks fresher. As he takes one last look, his attention shifts to a pair of scar-like markings on each wrist. Their placement is identical to where his sutures had been.

Immediately, the correlation turns his complexion pale. The eerie similarity is unnerving, and the man's comparable physique makes him feel like he is witnessing a clone. His eyes bulge as he watches the body crawl closer, further into the room. As each cadaver exhumes itself from beneath the bed, it becomes increasingly apparent that this encounter is more sinister than the preceding ones.

The disfigured bodies squirm and writhe as they complete their emergence from under the bed. Within minutes, A dozen or more corpses ominously stand motionless before him. Then, without warning, they disperse like a swarm of spiders fleeing an egg sac, scurrying across the room, and ascending the walls.

Each crack of their joints sends jitters through Adonis. He turns slowly toward the door, holding his breath and trying to avoid sudden movements.

Now scattered throughout the chamber, the cadavers emit low growls like feral animals as they prepare to hunt for him. Their macabre masks obstruct their sight, prompting them to rely on their sense of smell and hearing to detect any hint of movement.

Adonis is startled by one hanging from the wall beside him and gasps.

Its mouth opens, stretching its skin covering taut as it screeches to summon the others.

Adonis sprints toward the bedroom door, knowing that the closet will not be enough to keep him safe.

The corpse's call is immediately joined by the screeches of the other creatures, combining to create a deafening sound that reverberates through the walls. As it sends panic through his veins, he jimmies the handle faster. "Come on..." he says anxiously. He expects it to be locked, but it gives way, and he flings it open. Dashing from the room, he whirls around to slam the door and sees them charging aggressively.

With no way to lock the door from the outside, he holds onto the knob for dear life.

On the other side, the creatures grow desperate, snarling, their rabid fists pounding harder, rattling the wooden frame.

He struggles to keep it closed as his palms grow sweaty and his muscles quake. They viciously scratch and growl behind the door, exhibiting their relentless intent to reach him.

Quickly, he tries to tighten his slipping grip while frantically scanning the hallway for a place to hide.

There is just a single door.

Never having been inside, he does not know what lies behind it, but seeing no other option, he knows it is his only hope of finding a space that can lock from the inside.

Its white-painted wood calls to him.

Feeling his grasp slipping, he inhales deeply, releases the knob, and darts toward the door.

The creatures surge into the hallway behind him.

He grabs the brass knob and flings the entry open without looking back. As he peers into the pitch-black space, the screams of the corpses behind him become louder.

Darting into the abyss, he shuts the door and locks himself inside.

To him, the risk of the unknown is far better than being torn apart alive.

DEATH

Twelve

DON'T LET IT IN

In the darkness, everything appears sheathed by a veil of inky air. The pitch-black is ensured by a rubber seal installed around the doorframe, preventing any sliver of luminosity from entering.

In the murky confinement, environmental blindness renders Adonis's vision useless and his depth perception nonexistent. He stares at the darkness between him and the door. Even though it is in front of his nose, he imagines it is much farther away.

Uncertain of his surroundings, his mind runs wild, and adrenaline causes sweat to pool on his brow. He whispers, "Don't let them mess with your head."

Beyond the wooden barricade, the lifeless bodies swarm ferociously, scaling the walls and ceilings. Following his scent, they converge at the door and fiercely scratch and pound with their jagged nails, trying to gain entry.

With his eyes tightly shut, Adonis attempts to tune out the chaos; one breath at a time, he slows down his inhaling pace. As his racing heart calms, he tries to focus on his environment. His heightened senses of touch and hearing make each successive heartbeat resonate louder in his ears.

The doorframe rattles, and the wood flexes from the pressure of his aggressors. Even though he cannot see what is going on beyond the aperture, he imagines the hands of the faceless bodies becoming ragged with every forceful blow. The vivid imagery intensifies his anxiety as his mind delves into a dark realm, replaying each graphic image of the corpses' mutilated bodies like a slideshow through his mind.

Once again, hyperventilation takes hold, and his eyes snap open as the darkness dilates his pupils. His jaw muscles twitch as he fights to keep himself from blinking. "Think ... you gotta think... use your head," he whispers as he looks at the door; even though the creatures know where he is, he fears any change in sound will worsen their craze.

Suddenly, their screams and efforts to break the door down diminish. As their rambunctiousness calms down, he plans his next steps. Initially, the transition brings him comfort, but then he realizes that without the chaos, he has no excuse for his lack of attention to his surroundings. He knows he must now face what is behind him, and he swallows hard to keep the knot from forming in his throat.

With one final muffled screech, the noise outside ends, and Adonis moves closer, pressing his ear against the door.

Everything remains silent.

He finds their quick departure unsettling and takes a deep breath to calm his nerves. "You're fine. Everything's gonna be all right. You're good," he whispers.

After giving himself a moment to settle, he forces himself to turn around. Worried about running into something, he leaves his hands glued to his sides and carefully pivots. Instead of feeling relieved, his anxiety intensifies as he faces the opposite direction. Everything appears darker than before, adding to the turmoil in his mind.

The space is suddenly filled with the sound of a single drip.

His eyes dart from side to side; he does not know where to look. After all he has endured, the thought of haphazardly touching items he cannot see makes him cringe. He squints again to adjust his eyes to the dark but still struggles to find clarity.

Another drip echoes through the room.

Clenching his jaw, he reaches for the wall, and the texture of the wallpaper tickles his fingertips. He follows the grooves between the raised stripes, moving up and down the strands until his fingers hit a pair of buttons. "There you are," he says, smirking; his finger lingers. "Let's switch you on."

A slight *click* fills the air as he pushes the switch. The buzz of electricity draws his attention. His eyes flutter to acclimate as he shifts his gaze to the right, quickly spotting the warming bulb. The single basic brass-mounted fixture is affixed to the wall, and right beneath it sits an unframed antique oval-shaped mirror with a skewed reflection because of the silver backing being worn off.

As the bulb gathers power, the electrical hum levels out, and its essence shines brighter, reflecting against the glass and illuminating more of the room. The glow reveals a water-damaged, warped wooden floor beneath his loafers and a sticky yellow residue left by the missing tiles that previously surrounded a sink.

Glancing at his feet, he lightly runs the toe of his shoe over one of the glue markings near the sink basin. As it catches on an unleveled groove, he stops and, lowering himself to the floor, tries to get a better look.

The light dimly flickers, producing a glimmer off a broken piece of tile left behind; it has a washed burgundy hue. He carefully positions his hands on either side of the piece and lowers himself closer. "Huh. Interesting choice," he says, looking at the tiny shard; he cannot tell whether it is the tile's original color or a stain. Immediately, his mind jumps to the worst-case scenario, and he tries shaking any eerie notions out of his head.

Pushing himself to a squat, he attempts to distract himself by scanning the area. The air is permeated with an off-putting odor, a sharp, tangy scent that reminds him of pickles. His eyes drift to what he believes could be the source of the stench: the porcelain toilet in the corner of the small space. Keeping his gaze on the wooden seat and lid, he shuffles slightly closer.

Even though he's curious about what's hidden inside, he pauses. He cannot recall whether he has used the bathroom since being detained, highlighting the gaps in his memory.

As he rises to his feet, a sudden surge of dizziness over-whelms him, and he grips the wooden door of the sink cabinet to steady himself. "I must be dehydrated." He says.

The faint sound of trickling water echoes throughout the room. Unsure of where it is coming from, he wants to follow the noise, but his head becomes heavy, leaving his attention on the commode.

The porcelain's dull exterior displays evidence of wear and tear, indicating that it has been heavily used. As he stares at the details, he is overcome by fatigue and compul-sively yawns.

The lingering acidic smell makes his eyes itch, and his nostrils burn. "I don't get how anyone can deal with that crap. Smells like I've been soaking in a pickle jar," he says, slurring and not making much sense. Each of his words irritates his throat. He clings onto the cabinet door, grunt-ing with exertion as he struggles to stay upright.

Repositioning his hands on the sides of the sink, he focuses his attention on the drain. A dark stain surrounds it, etched into the mineralized porcelain's surface.

His legs weaken beneath him, and his eyes wince. "What...is happening... what is wrong... with me," he says, disjointed.

A wave of nausea envelops him as he glances at his re-flection in the mirror, unsure if he can hold back the acidic bile rising in his throat. He quickly turns to the toilet, yet his reflection keeps looking straight ahead, revealing a contradiction to his perceived reality.

His sickness overcomes him, turning his face green. Pushing himself away from the sink, he rushes to the toilet bowl and falls to the floor, unable to keep his balance.

The dark character's eyes follow him from the mirror.

A trail of whispers fills the room as he scrambles to open the lid. "Don't let it in ... don't let it in," they say. Continuing their repetitive chant, each sentence becomes more aggressive than the last.

The voices sound like a pounding tambourine, exacerbating his headache. His entire body convulses as he tries to hold in his sickness. "Leave me—" Before he can finish his sentence, the stomach acid makes it to his mouth, forcing his dialogue to stop.

The heckling voices grow louder, creating an overwhelming tension in the room. The air thickens with anticipation, signifying an ominous presence lurking deep in the space.

Adonis vomits uncontrollably, his body racked with convulsions, as the voices merge, one after the other, transforming into a demonic cacophony.

His fingers grip the lid's wooden edges, and he flips it open mid-heave. Having been sealed up for some time, an overwhelming smell of sour gas is unleashed from the toilet bowl, pelting Adonis in the face.

The blended whispers become cackling screams as the dark face in the mirror transforms, its lips curling into a sneer and stare fading into soulless black holes.

Despite his burning eyes, Adonis can't halt his impending sickness and continues to hunch over the gassy bowl while trying to ignore the pain. The fumes provoke the state of his eyes to worsen. He remains oblivious that the corrosive gas's effects are much more severe than just burning eyes and swollen lids, as it gradually erodes his pupils and causes permanent blindness.

The warm light above the mirror flickers on cue, and the cackling stops.

Unable to see, Adonis gasps for air as the eerie silence of his suffering surrounds him.

The man's mouth appears warped in the mirror as he speaks. "With his sacrifice, I call for the last veil of the spirit realm to be lifted. My son's body will pay for my karmic debt, washing my soul clean. He failed to appreciate the value of his life, rationalizing his decisions with excuses rather than using his lessons to cultivate his resilience and determination. I am giving him the purpose of his destiny, a gift he'll never forget. With the exchange of hands, I transfer the weight of my deeds onto him. With his eyes vacant and his voice silenced, he will spend his days solely existing to repay my karmic debt, releasing me from the burden of my atonement." he says; his profound whisper shakes the room.

As his image dissipates, his chanting echoes through the room, bouncing off the walls and enveloping everything within it, sealing the ritual and Adonis's fate. The malevolent words possess a spellbinding effect on Adonis, leaving him paralyzed as the biting fumes burn his throat, eroding the tissue of his vocal cords and rendering him speechless.

Suddenly, a loud knock on the door disrupts the chant's rhythm. As he struggles to break free from the invisible grip on his body, he strains to listen to the noise coming from outside the door.

The knock turns into a frantic pounding, rattling the wood. Through his delirium and pain, he distinguishes a muffled voice resonating from the hallway, coordinated with the aggressive thuds. "We know you are hiding in there," A male voice says authoritatively. The man delivers another barrage of forceful knocks and raises his voice even louder.

"Open up!" He shouts.

Adonis feels a throbbing pain in his head as the invisible force continues to press down on his body, causing tears to well up in his eyes. As they trickle down his cheeks, he wants to call for help and, opening his mouth, tries to scream. "He—help," he struggles to say. Even though he imagines the words exiting his lips, nothing comes out.

The resistance holding him down grows heavier by the minute, almost crushing his body. He knows he has little time. Giving one last attempt, he fights it with everything he has left. He turns around to face the door, his neck veins bulging with effort. His overexertion makes him froth from the mouth. Refusing to submit, he crawls toward the voice, believing it to be his only hope.

The pounding quickens against the entrance.

As he reaches the halfway point across the small room, he hears a faint whispering in his ear. It is the man that haunts his reflection.

Adonis stops crawling, paralyzed with fear. His trembling worsens, his arms giving out from beneath him, and he collapses to the floor.

The dark voice hauntingly drifts into oblivion. "Welcome to your new beginning and my freedom." He says.

The words strike a nerve, making his heart race and leaving him feeling like it will pound through the wall of his chest.

Unexpectedly, a resounding boom fills the room as the door is aggressively kicked open, just missing his fingertips, as it crashes into the wall. Adonis frantically covers his head with his hands to protect himself. Still unable to see, he timidly lifts his chin, directing his attention to the sound.

He flinches as a burly grip wraps around his arms and forcefully yanks him into the hallway. The act prompts Adonis to relive the traumatic experience of his captor pulling him by his ankles, and he frantically struggles to break free.

The grasp tightens as an assertive voice shouts, "Looks like formaldehyde in the bathroom!" Then, lowering his voice, he redirects his attention to securing Adonis's hands behind his back. "You are under arrest," he says.

Helplessly, with his cheek smashed against the floor, he recognizes the words and general timbre of the voice. The idea of being at the mercy of a police officer makes him break out in a cold sweat. As he struggles to escape, memories of his unpleasant experiences with the police flood his mind.

Clothed in his all-blue uniform, the officer's pallid complexion is tinged with a hue of red due to the forceful effort of breaking down the door. Demonstrating no leniency for Adonis's escape attempt, he adjusts his weight onto him, immobilizing him on the ground and securing his hands behind his back with handcuffs.

Exhausted, Adonis takes a deep breath and complies. Regardless of the situation, he feels his prayers have been answered: he has been rescued. As the metal cuffs tighten, he finds the experience is more aggressive than expected, and the unforgiving edges cut into his skin; the pain makes him wince.

The sheriff drags him to his feet. "You are under arrest," he says, patting Adonis's pockets for belongings. Hearing a crinkle, he reaches inside his pocket, and his fingers fish out a small piece of paper. He quickly glances at the ticket while keeping a firm grip on the handcuffs, trying to decipher the handwritten text. Only two letters are legible. "A.G., that's your name, is it?" He says.

The words send a shiver down Adonis's spine, and he frantically shakes his head no. As he tries to speak, he is overcome by a suffocating feeling in his throat.

The officer shows indifference to his response and slips the paper into his pocket. "You are under arrest for trespassing," he says. The words render Adonis motionless.

Hearing no response, the sheriff becomes agitated and forcefully drives his knee into his back. "What was that? Did you say something? You understand me, boy?" he asks.

Adonis grimaces as pain shoots through the back of his ribcage. As he struggles to catch his breath, he acknowledges he has broken into the home with an affirming nod.

The officer snickers. "Good boy," he says.

Adonis relinquishes all control, resting on the assurance that he can explain once his voice returns. He feels anything is better than remaining on the houseboat.

With a resounding grunt, the officer forcefully drags him down the hall.

Adonis shudders at the sound of approaching footsteps. Another officer is charging in their direction, heading straight toward them. His reddish-colored stubble contradicts his pale, colorless complexion; he looks shaken. With a frantic stop in front of them, he salutes, and his hand skittishly hits the stiff brim of his blue hat, almost knocking it off his head. "Uh ... Sheriff... sir..." he says.

Annoyed, the sheriff answers, "Yes, deputy?"

The young man stumbles over his words while trying to catch his breath. "I—I think w ... we have a bigger issue on our hands," he says, barely able to get his words out.

The sheriff finds his reaction laughable and responds with an eye roll. "Jesus Christ, deputy, you got to man up and get a hold of yourself. Pull yourself together," he says with exasperation, gripping the handcuffs tightly as he guides Adonis down the hallway.

The deputy races after them, trying to catch up. "But ... there's..."

They make it to the end of the short hall, and despite his efforts, the deputy cannot stop them in time. They come to a sudden stop in the kitchen. "What in God's name?" the sheriff says, plugging his nose; he looks at the open freezer.

Staring back from the shelf is a woman's severed head with a patchwork skin covering. The rest of the compartment is filled with packages of various shapes and sizes, wrapped in black garbage bags, and secured with brown shipping tape.

"That's not all, sir," the deputy says, clearing his throat and speaking faster. "As I followed the scrape marks across the floor, I discovered what appeared to be a torture chamber in the closet. Honest to God, I do not know what kind of sick person could do this, but ... but..." His trauma gets the best of him, and he stammers as his eyes nervously dart around the room.

The sheriff's demeanor shifts. "Shit," he says. He places his hand on Adonis's back and gives him a forceful shove, causing him to stumble forward. His eyes quickly survey the living room, scanning the scene. Suddenly, his glare fixates on a small, empty tinfoil packet on the sofa. In an attempt to grab the deputy's attention, he nods toward it. "You know what that means, don't you?"

His motion is met with a blank stare from the deputy, indicating his cluelessness. "N-no sir," he says.

With confidence, the sheriff puffs his chest out and explains. "That's a dead giveaway that drugs were involved, which all makes sense with the wet set of clothes hung out to dry on the porch. It is common for them to hallucinate and strip buck-naked," he says. "Based on my extensive experience, I've found that nine times out of ten, drug-abusing drifters are criminals."

Even though he's unsure if he agrees, the deputy quickly nods. "So, what should we do?" he asks.

"Once we get him outside, you get on the radio and call in someone else to deal with this mess," the sheriff replies.

The sheriff directs his gaze toward the propped-open front door and, using his hand, swats at a fly hovering around his face. "Let's speed this up. It's hot as hell in here, and I have the criminal in custody. Our part is done," he says while guiding Adonis toward the exit.

Then, with a smirk, he glances back at the deputy and chuckles. "Between us men, my wife's making one of my favorites for dinner, chicken-n-dumplings, and I will be in the doghouse if I'm late again. The last thing I want to do is sleep on the couch tonight."

"Whatever you say, boss." He replies, Laughing nervously. The deputy takes one last look at the open freezer and becomes captivated by the hypnotic hum of the flies congregating nearby. Upon realizing his distraction, he hastily rushes to catch up and simultaneously radios into headquarters.

Albert is waiting for them on the dock, wearing the same fishing gear from the previous day. The blazing sun burns his skin, charring his forehead as he desperately shields his eyes from the glare.

The police officers make eye contact with him as they lead the man away in handcuffs. Albert hurries toward them but hesitates when he sees Adonis's clothing. The sight of the suit triggers a memory for him - he recognizes it as his father's. Nervously stepping back, he finds it difficult to find his words. "Is ... is that the guy who broke in?" he asks, trying to act normal.

With only sound to rely on, Adonis panics, hearing another voice added to the mix. As he fights to keep track of everything happening, he twists and turns, seeking their attention as he struggles to speak, but despite his efforts, he remains voiceless.

Annoyed by his jarring movement, the sheriff smacks his back. "Yup, sure is him. He is mute. He must have done serious damage to his brain with all those drugs," he says, with a hint of disgust in his voice.

Albert notices the panic etched on Adonis's face and recognizes a sense of familiarity in his eyes.

The sheriff gives Adonis another hard shove to enforce compliance. "Yeah, and that's not all. Based on what we found, he had taken up residence on your boat long before the storm. He just hid it well until now. He probably got a little too full of himself, which made him careless, so he got caught this time. It's obvious he's been living there for a while and doing some really messed up shit. Maybe even killed some folks," he says. He grabs Adonis's shoulders and gives them a sarcastic shake, drawing attention to his outfit, then laughs and says, "Looks like he dressed up for the occasion."

With his eyes fixed on Adonis, the deputy follows suit, wiggling his shoulders awkwardly while chiming in. "Trying to look like a high-class individual." He chuckles.

The sheriff's glare prompts him to straighten his tone and stop speaking. "In any case, you can breathe a sigh of relief knowing that this lowlife won't be prowling the streets, stealing your belongings, or doing God knows what else. He'll be locked up with his kind in jail by supper," he says.

As Albert studies Adonis's face, he cannot help but feel a sense of unease at the unsettling resemblance to his father. "Did you get a name?" he asks.

The officer is ready to hit the road and responds brusquely, clearly irritated by the questioning. "Yeah, he goes by A.G.," he says.

Hearing the initials makes Albert nauseous. Not only do they belong to him, but also to his father. Paralyzed with fear, his eyes remain fixated on the man they have in handcuffs, realizing it could have easily been him.

While roughing up Adonis, the sheriff further boasts, "Since the guy refuses to talk, we searched his pockets for ID. As expected, he had no wallet. Luckily, we found a dry-cleaning receipt in his coat pocket with his name on it."

Abruptly chiming in, the deputy gestures over his shoulder toward the houseboat, eager to add his input.

"You are lucky that thing doesn't have a motor on it, or boy, oh, boy, he would have been long gone," he says, chuckling.

Not knowing what to say, Albert remains silent.

The sheriff squints as he analyzes his face, suspicious of his lack of response. "You know, it's strange to me—we may have just caught a killer hiding out on your dad's old houseboat, and you're not saying a damn word. You're just standing there, silent, with a look on your face like you've seen a ghost," he says.

The deputy slowly feels an interrogation coming on and moves next to his boss to join in. "Yeah, it's pretty damn strange," he says, chiming in.

Albert, desperate to shield his family, suppresses his anxiety and lets out a forced laugh at the officer's suspicion. "Oh, no, there is nothing wrong, sir. I'm in shock, to be honest. I have never seen an actual killer up close before," he says.

Sensing Adonis's discomfort, the sheriff tightens his grasp and grins. "Well, that makes sense for a small-town man like you. I'd say we're done here. We had better hit the road; it's a long drive back to county headquarters. Sure would be easier if these small towns had their own police," he says, motioning for his subordinate to follow him while leading Adonis down the dock.

Halfway down the pier, he turns and shouts, "Oh, I almost forgot something!" Albert's stomach drops, certain that this is the moment he's been dreading. The sheriff adds, "The houseboat might be off-limits for a day or two. Police protocol and such. The others should arrive some-time later today. If I were you, I wouldn't go inside until we get someone out here to clean up the mess."

Any remaining police involvement is strictly protocol. As far as they are concerned, the case is closed with the killer in custody. Stunned by their quick departure and lack of securing the scene, Albert nods. "Yes, sir," he replies.

Albert's eyes shift away as he feels a wave of guilt wash over him, noticing Adonis's attempt to hinder his movement by dragging his shoes on the wooden planks leading to the car. Abruptly, the sheriff whistles, calling for the deputy. He runs toward him, grasps an arm, and helps drag Adonis to the police cruiser.

Albert's gaze fixates on the peacefulness of the houseboat's exterior; he cannot understand how an object can ruin so many lives. As Adonis and the police reach the end of the pier, a wave of relief washes over him, and his body relaxes.

The sheriff forces Adonis into the back of the patrol car and slams the door behind him. He notices the row of shops across the street and turns back toward Albert, laughing. "Hey, Albert!" he shouts.

Albert startles at the sound and swiftly pivots, sweat trickling down his forehead. "Yes, sir?" he shouts back while nervously watching the sheriff point to the bait shop sign across the street.

With a laugh, the officer motions toward the buildings. "You said you own that shop over there, right?" he asks.

Immediately, Albert thinks of the shop's title. "Shit," he whispers, his heart racing with fear as he waits for them to arrest him as well, sure that they have connected the name to the initials discovered in the suspect's pocket.

The sheriff shouts louder, "I like the play on words!
Gill! It's like fish's gills ... It's funny. That's funny!" His
boisterous voice echoes against the swamp water.

Confused by his statement, Albert quickly looks at his
shop to determine what he is talking about. At that moment, he sees it. The storm has caused several letters to fall
off, resulting in the sign now reading *Gill Bait Shop*.

He looks at it with disbelief.

Amid his bewilderment, the sheriff approaches the driver's side door and shouts over the car's roof to the deputy.
"One thing I've learned over the years is you can tell a lot
about a man's character by his sense of humor. Trust me,
you can take that to the bank."

As Albert watches their doors close, a shiver rolls down
his spine, and he forces a smile. Seeing the vehicle driving
away seems surreal as he gives a single wave. He slowly turns to face the houseboat, his tone becoming bit-
ter. "Even when you're dead, I'm still dealing with your
bullshit." He says. Clenching his jaw, he begrudgingly approaches the eyesore and enters through the open door.

Inside, the stench of death wafts through the air.

He's noticed a strange odor in the area during his rare
visits over the past decade, but it's far worse this time,
forcing him to hold his breath while on his mission. As
he passes through the kitchen, his eyes dart around the
space before landing on the open freezer door. Until now,
he had never looked inside the appliance, so he did not
know about its horrifying contents, but he knew his father's character, leading him to wonder who was really to
blame for the gruesome acts. He avoids investigating the
freezer further and instead focuses on scanning the room

for anything that could incriminate him. Considering the officers' reactions, he knows the investigative work will be careless and more of a technicality, but with more officers due to arrive, he wants to avoid tempting fate.

His anxiety hinders his ability to reason, prompting him to impulsively snatch anything that he believes may incriminate him. Only one item commands his attention-his father's ashes. He worries his fingerprints may be on the container from when he first placed them on the boat.

As he heads toward the exit, can in hand, he passes a kitchen drawer that is slightly ajar with the corner of a photo sticking out. He seizes it, and his mind races as he rapidly scans the black-and-white picture. It is an image of his father embracing a young boy, and assuming it is him, he takes it, too. Grasping the items, he swiftly exits without looking back.

He promptly makes his way to the edge of the dock and stands momentarily in contemplation, staring over the water. Albert takes one last look at the ashes, then hurls the can into the air, aiming it toward the bayou.

Against the backdrop of the blue sky, the tin tumbles through the air, sending its contents flying, including a voodoo doll buried deep beneath the ashes. The doll's eyes and mouth are marked with an X and sharpened matchsticks pierce each spot where Adonis was injured. The most distinguishing characteristic is the hair that embellishes the body.

Albert is too focused on resentfully glaring at the cloud of ashes blowing in the wind to notice anything else.

Suddenly, he senses someone watching him and turns around.

A woman, her skin gracefully showing signs of age, stands at the end of the dock, waving at him; her head is wrapped with a bright yellow scarf that matches her flowing dress. The woman is his mother.

Her face exudes happiness with a broad smile as she holds a well-worn leather-bound book.

"I'll be right there, Momma. Go on, get back inside now; it's not safe with all this debris around," he says, motioning with his hand.

She nods as she continues to smile.

With a heavy sigh, he glances at the photo in his hand. Shaking his head, he says, "That look on my face says it all. Even as a child, I didn't trust the man."

He finds it odd, considering he never recalls coming across a picture of himself with a similar haircut, but anything is possible in a family of secrets.

Albert shrugs, then flings the image into the murky swamp, feeling a weight lifted off his shoulders as he rids himself of yet another painful reminder of his toxic father.

His mother tightens her grip on the book and, observing him, brings it to her lips, kissing the worn cover. "Kouri lapli, tonbe larivye," she says in a whisper, "It took the grace of Bondye and ten years to prepare for this day, the day that sets us free."

She is overwhelmed by the sun's splendor, and a tear trickles down her cheek.

Then, catching sight of the houseboat, she redirects her attention and spits on the ground, symbolically removing negative thoughts about her husband. A chuckle escapes her lips as she recalls him lying on his deathbed. "He demanded I rid him of his karma to allow him a *peaceful rest*. Ha! Fool!" She says.

With a voluminous gasp, her eyes widen, and her voice deepens as she channels the spirits, preparing to unleash the details of his sentencing: "His debt is too large for a single lifetime; it demands sixty-five years of penance by two souls to be cleared. Both dividing the sentence must be bound by blood, one in the realm of the living and one in the realm of the dead. The responsible one will aimlessly wander, decomposing and devoid of purpose, his nostrils filling soil and dust, spiritually anchored to the earth, while the young man will remain speechless and trapped within his iron cage."

As she finishes, she exhales heavily and lowers the book to rest against her heart. "Despite that young man's flaws, my heart aches for his sacrifice. But what's done is done," she says.

With her head bowed in reverence, she whispers, "Thanks be to Bondy for releasing us from the weight of the man's karmic debt."

The water swarms around the picture. Little does Albert know that his thought about the hair's style was accurate; although his hair was never cut that way, Adonis's was. The photo was taken to mark his first birthday, following the custom of cutting his curls for the first time and preserving the locks.

Her husband cunningly tucked away the strands, concealing them among the clutter of a kitchen drawer on his houseboat. He was confident in his wife's ignorance of his indiscretions, but his volatile character stopped her from challenging him, not her obliviousness. Instead of acting on impulse, she exhibited patience, biding her time until his demise before boarding the houseboat to seek an item to help craft the doll for the ritual. It was at that moment when she stumbled upon the picture and hair side by side, instantly recognizing their significance.

Albert steps further away, trying to hold back his tears. As a drop escapes, it tumbles down his cheek and drips between the wooden slats of the dock, making its way into the swamp.

After one final sniffle, his thoughts drift to his mother, who patiently waits for him. He swiftly brushes away his tears to prevent her from worrying. Putting on a smile, he walks toward her; each of his heavy steps rattles the wooden structure and stirs the water.

With every ripple, the photo is pulled deeper into the swamp, joining the can and doll in their final resting place at the bottom of the murky abyss.

A peaceful bayou is all that remains.

GITTE TAMAR

Brigitte, "Gitte," Tamar was born in a small rural Oregon town. Growing up, she was enthralled by scary tales featuring poetic tones and consistently gravitated towards writing darkened narratives. She graduated from Jesuit High School in Portland and attended Texas Christian University in Fort Worth, Texas until she won the title of Miss Oregon USA in 2015.

Once she finished competing in the Miss USA televised program, she received her business degree from Southern New Hampshire University. Then, her MA in Studies of Law from the University of Southern California, followed by graduate certificates in business law and entertainment law and industries.

As an author, she explores the harsh realities of social issues faced by today's generations. This includes the dark outcomes brought on by peer pressure, addiction, homelessness, mental illness, childhood trauma, and abuse. She feels it is essential to share narratives that refrain from sugarcoating the topics society tends to shy away from.

Many of Tamar's published works have been reviewed by critics and production companies, including BroadwayWorld. Her most recent novel, "Hel," released in July

2023, was featured by Mystery Tribune as one of July's best crime and mystery books to watch for.

Also, her most recent children's picture book, "The Lonely Ghost," is a recipient of the prestigious Mom's Choice Award.